What Would Oprah Do?

Erin Emerson

ISBN-13: 978-0615880488 (King Literary Group)
ISBN-10: 0615880487

This is a work of fiction. Names, characters, businesses, places, events and incidents are either the products of the author's imagination or used in a fictitious manner. Any resemblance to actual persons, living or dead, or actual events is purely coincidental. This work is not endorsed by Oprah Winfrey.

Strength shows not only in the ability to persist, but in the ability to start over.

F. Scott Fitzgerald

To my Dad, who taught me to be brave.

CHAPTER 1

Dear Oprah,

In just four months I have realized that I can unintentionally give a room full of people food poisoning in an hour, get a charitable organization to ask me not to volunteer again, kill any plant I attempt to care for within a month, and turn 50 yards of fabric into something no one would wear. I'm not proud of this, especially since I'm telling the woman who could turn a room full of straw into gold. I'm not one of those crazy people who thinks you have a magic wand. However, I do have to admit that if I ever met you, and you pulled one out, I wouldn't be the least bit surprised.

I know you're not going to read this; some intern might and decide that I'm nuts and block all future emails from me. Yet for some reason I get a little hope by writing to you. This is my way of throwing it out there. You found your way in this world, and by God, I'm looking for mine. I'm not asking you for anything. I'm tired of people asking you for things, so I can imagine how you must feel about it. You had a show on recession, and how people are making it through the economic downturn. There was a woman on your show, about to lose her house, and as you tried to get her to talk about her situation and what she was going to do to get through it, her voice cracked and she started to cry. I feel bad saying this, but I think she was crying out of shock: 'What? Oprah, I thought you put me on the show to be my personal salvation army! You want me to talk about what I'm going to do? I really am going to cry if you aren't going to pay my mortgage!' I swear that was what she was thinking. All I could think was 'Oh Oprah, this woman came on the show expecting you to save the day!' I bet that happens to you all the time.

Now for the part that is going to make the intern reading this decide that I'm crazy. I play a game in my head, like the people who play the lottery: where you think about what you would do if you won. I don't play the lottery. I can never remember to buy a ticket. The game I play is 'what if Oprah adopted me?' I know it sounds nuts, but it helps me stay positive, thinking about how my whole life could be different, and all the stupid problems I have would be gone. It's hard to sort out your whole life when you haven't figured out the basics. Thank you for being there, so I can have my own silly daydream that gets me through the day. Sometimes I need that, even if it's just 5 minutes of imagining that it could all miraculously be fine in the end.

Regards,

Cate

P.S. I may have underestimated how long I spend playing 'If Oprah adopted me'. It's probably closer to twenty minutes on the days that it's really hard to get out of bed. Also, if you decide you want to adopt a 32 year old white girl, please let me know.

I was sitting in my softest pajamas randomly looking up old friends from high school on Facebook. They all have pictures of happy babies, which I don't necessarily want. There are pictures of husbands too, and I would like one of those but that hasn't worked out yet. While I looked at one of the pictures where the focal point was undoubtedly supposed to be her little girls playing in the yard, it hit me. All I can see is the yard, the nice big fenced in yard with green grass, and a big shiny stainless grill. You can almost smell barbecue and hear a little laughter in the distance. And the only thing I can think is that I'm all alone and I have nothing, which isn't exactly true.

I have friends, and my sister and parents. Technically, I really do have nothing. I have a mortgage on a condo, an interest-only loan in a sinking market, so I'm no closer to owning it than I was 6 years ago when I bought it. I have a car, which I recently found out I'm upside-down on, so I definitely don't own that. That blows my mind, that I couldn't sell it without giving someone money to take it from me. You can add that to the long list of things that make me feel ridiculous at this very moment. Anyway, back to the pictures, you can just see it on their faces that they don't look at that yard and wonder how the hell they're going to pay for it, which is what I do with the one bedroom, one bath, 700 square feet of space that I call home.

I've always been happy with my life, being a single girl with a career, making my own choices, but now that I look at all of my old friends' pictures, I'm jealous. I envy that they're not worrying about the fundamentals, like their electric bill or what kind of life to have. Sure, they're probably thinking about their kids' college tuitions and what not, but I don't even have a savings plan for myself anymore, and I don't know when or how I ever will again.

They say that two can live almost as cheaply as one. Maybe if there had been a second income, I'd have something to show for all the years I've busted my ass just trying to make a life for myself. Here I am with nothing, trying to figure out where my money went. I know where most of it went: maintenance, going out, entertainment, drinking and smoking. I have nothing to show for it, unless some future doctor's visit reveals some damage that I have yet to find out about.

I don't even have nice jewelry. The most valuable thing that I own outright is an unworn Gucci dress that I bought three years ago, when I read in a magazine "10 Things You Should Have By the Time You're Thirty" that said you should always have a formal black dress, so you're ready to go at a moment's notice to a fancy event. Now I could never wear it at a moment's notice because I would have to lose fifteen pounds to fit in it without looking like a black stuffed sausage.

Maybe I should lose those fifteen pounds and start going to events in my fancy black dress, shopping for a husband. I had always planned on the right man coming along, and marrying for love. Now that I've lost my job, discovered that I don't have potential in anything I've tried since, and sit around wishing Oprah would adopt me, it may be time to rethink things.

I have to face the facts. I have no idea what to do with my life and the only thing that gives me hope is writing letters to Oprah. I really believe that she tries to do good in this world, and it's just nice to imagine that she lets me move into one of her houses and gives me some sort of stipend or general relief so I can find my purpose. Right now I don't have a clue what I'm supposed to do with my life, nor do I have the luxury of time to sort it out since I have bills to pay.

When I got laid off I thought it was going to be easy. Two days before I lost my job, I realized that marketing was not what I was supposed to do with my life. I had felt it growing in me for months, some gnawing dissatisfaction. The weekends went by so fast, and the dread on Sunday night had grown to dread on Sunday morning, at the mere thought of going to work. I was on my way to meet a friend for drinks, a friend I hadn't seen in a long time, where you have to try to explain what you actually do for work, since they think they're interested until you start telling them. Somewhere on the drive over there, it hit me like a ton of bricks, *I can't do this anymore*. I was so certain that I told her as soon as I got there that it was time for me to do something else with my life, although I didn't know what. I did know a few things: I wanted to feel good about my existence again, instead of my current purpose of figuring out how to separate consumers from their money. I knew that I needed to do something that I could be passionate about, instead of trying to hang on to every weekend and holiday for dear life.

I got home that night, and prayed, although I'm not sure to whom, that I would find something else to do with my life, the right path for me, ASAP. So two days later when I got laid off, corporate downsizing that no one was expecting, I thought it was divine intervention. I had saved up just enough money to pay my bare necessities for five months. I figured that since somehow God had immediately intervened and changed my work situation, surely I could sort out where to go from there in five months. Besides, at the time I thought I had a lot of potential. Sure I was stunned and freaking out a bit when I found out that my position was being eliminated. I even cried when I found out I was only getting two weeks' severance pay. As soon as I left my meeting with human resources, I did what any single girl would do. I texted Jill to meet for emergency cocktails. Not only is Jill my closest friend who knows all the details of my life, she's also the best at commiserating.

We went to the pub near her apartment. It's not exactly a great spot, but as one of the last people who has yet to smarten up and give up smoking; it's one of the few places where I can indulge my filthy habit. Since Jill wasn't losing her job and able to run out the office door, I got to the bar before she did. However, being the great friend that she is, she left as soon as she could and was there in thirty minutes. I was sitting at the bar, already on my second beer. Jill rushed in, hugging me before sitting on the stool beside mine. "I'm so sorry. Are you ok?" She asked, eyeing the mascara trail that I hadn't even thought to wipe off my face.

"Yeah, I think I am." I nodded, still unable to fully wrap myself around it. After my first beer, it had sunk in somewhat.

"Really? And you're drinking beer, not a martini?" She looked incredulous.

I said, "I figured this was an occasion worthy of carbs."

Jill used a cocktail napkin and condensation from my beer bottle to wipe off the mascara streaks. She said, "This is why you should wear waterproof mascara every day. You never know when you'll need it. Where's Kay?"

I shrugged, "Probably on her way, but I told her not to come."

Jill said, "She's your sister! Why would you tell her not to come?"

"By the time she could leave, traffic would already be bad. And if you really think about it, I lost a job that I hate. I mean, yeah, I also lost the paycheck that I busted my ass for, but I wanted to leave anyway."

"I thought you would be a wreck! What the hell happened?" Jill motioned for the bartender to bring her a beer.

"I don't even know where to start. When I came back from lunch, there was this random meeting on my calendar for a client review. I knew something was weird because it was obviously scheduled by Barbara, my boss, since it was on my calendar without me accepting an invite. Also, it was in the boardroom. We never use the boardroom unless the conference rooms aren't available, or we need the big projector. I tried to get in touch with Barbara to see if I needed to bring anything, but she wasn't in her office and never replied to my email. I would have thought more of it if Barbara wasn't always such a mess, but I just figured she probably wasn't paying attention when she booked the room. Speaking of, Cheers!"

"Cheers to what?" she asked.

"No more stupid ass Barbara!"

"Ah," Jill answered as she clinked the top of her beer bottle on mine. "I have to say, you're taking this a lot better than I would have thought." I could feel her eyes on me, looking for some indication that under my good cheer tears were on the way.

"Well it is what it is. Anyway, when I started walking down the hall to the boardroom, there were random people from different teams going that way too. I figured we were probably moving accounts around or something, but I knew when I got to the door. Barbara was sitting at the end of the table, looking like somebody had died or something and the big clue - Jennifer from HR was sitting in the corner. I don't know when he flew in, but our CEO was there too, so I knew shit was going down."

"Oh no, HR and CEO in the same room is always a bad sign! What was everyone else doing?"

"They looked like cattle, herded to a slaughter house, trailing in the door. At that point, you'd have to be an idiot to not figure it out. Oh, and Mr. CEO started his little speech with 'I'm not happy to be here today…' Then he said 'As we all know the economy has been affecting our clients', and this shit is verbatim, 'now the economy is affecting each of you.' Can you believe that?"

Jill was shaking her head. She said, "Oh my God! That is so tacky."

"Oh wait, it gets worse. He went on and on about how hard it was for him and that it had almost ruined his Christmas knowing that he was going to come here this week and let us go, like we should feel sorry for him or something."

"Asshole!" she said a little too loudly. "Then what?"

"That's about it. They handed out packets to everybody, with our individual separation details. I only get two weeks' severance since I've only been there a year. I never should have left Headlines. At least then I would have gotten a decent severance package. Anyway, we have to work for the next week to transfer over our accounts. And oh my God, I can't believe I almost forgot this! He said that we needed to realize that it was hard for the people who were staying too, and we needed to be positive during the transition time to minimize survivor's guilt!"

Jill's face reflected the indignance that I wished I had the energy to muster. "Seriously Cate, that's bullshit. How does someone get to be a CEO without having a little diplomacy?"

"Beats the hell out of me." I answered. "Now I just have to figure out what to do with the rest of my life. You know, after I've done my part to reduce survivor's guilt."

"Well, you don't have to figure that out tonight. Give it a few days, then start sending your resume out. I'm sure you'll find something in no time."

"With everybody downsizing, never mind the holidays, it won't be easy. And besides, this wasn't how I thought it would happen, but it's time for me to do something else. I hate my job."

"You don't hate your job. You have a shitty boss. You know as well as I do that it doesn't matter what job you have, if your boss sucks, the job sucks."

"I know, but it's not just her. Seriously, I hate my job, the whole industry. I decided that on Monday and prayed for change."

"You prayed? Since when do you pray?" Jill's head was cocked to the side so far that it's easy to see why she goes to a chiropractor.

"Since two days ago. I don't know why you think it's weird; you're the one who goes to church" I said.

"Exactly, I go to church, but you don't even have a religion!"

"Just because I don't have everything labeled, doesn't mean I don't have my own thing. Anyway, the other day I prayed for God to show me something else to do with my life, that I wanted to have a purpose and boom, today I get laid off. It's a sign."

"How is that a sign?" she asked.

"Well, what are the odds that on the rare occasion I pray, I ask for something very specific, and the process starts happening two days later?" Jill started peeling the label off her beer. "I'm just saying the God I can't completely define, but fully believe in, wouldn't set me up for failure. This has to be part of the plan somehow."

I remembered the moment I had realized this on some level during the layoff meeting, when I almost felt relief. I had only cried because I was stunned and scared.

"Ok, so I guess it's a good thing that you're not falling apart…" she said.

"That may happen tomorrow. I don't know, but if you think about it, you're only born with two fears: loud noises and falling. Everything else you learn along the way. I can't be scared of what I don't know. It's ridiculous. If you think about it, you never really know anything. And everything that you think of as security is just secure as far as you know. My future could be anything, and if I can rule out that my future won't be a job that I dread and despise, there's nothing to be upset about, just some details to sort through."

Jill stared at my face. "Did you take Xanax or something?" she asked.

"I wish. I think the last beer helped, after the first two took the edge off. I don't know. I think it's time for me to do something else, and now I'm being forced to by circumstance."

I started to get excited thinking about all the unknown possibilities. "Let's celebrate change!" I yelled. "Who knows? They didn't lay off everybody, maybe a fourth of our office. Maybe yesterday I wasn't included in that group, and today I was."

Jill said, "If you want to celebrate, we'll celebrate. You're right. Who knows? Maybe you're onto something, but please don't pray for change for me." I laughed with an ease that I hadn't felt in a long time. We stayed for hours, and by the time Kay got there, I was drunk. The drunker I got, the more I felt like celebrating, like a weight had been lifted. God had a plan, for me.

CHAPTER 2

Dear Oprah,

I'm writing to you because you may be the only person who will understand that my being laid off last week is a good thing. You have said before that getting fired is a blessing because the universe is telling you to change course. I heard you tell how you were fired from your first anchor job. After that, you got an offer to have your own talk show. That worked out very well for you, you have your own network now! I feel like my future will be better too, even if on a smaller scale. I believe it. Unlike last year when I found out that my fiancé James was cheating on me. After a month I started telling people that I just felt grateful, like I'd dodged a bullet by finding out before I married him. Really I was alternating between drinking my dinner, and sitting on my kitchen floor, crying and eating saltines while "I Will Survive" was on continuous replay. This is totally different, and I know in my heart that this is the beginning of something great. Thank you for being a shining example of how 'losing' a job can be the way to gain your life.

Regards,

Cate

P.S. And to think, at one point you were upset that instead of you, Monica Kauffman got the anchor job in my home town, Atlanta.

I feel great. This morning I woke up without a hangover, despite all of my celebrating last night. I pushed the button on my coffee maker, since I am the last person alive who doesn't have a timer on the coffee maker. Normally I stand there waiting for it to brew, because I can't shower until I feel caffeine coursing through my veins. Today I took a shower while it brewed.

In the car I found myself laughing at the jokes on the radio morning show and singing along to every song. When I pulled into the parking lot, I texted Kay and Jill: "Thanks again for last night. No hangover, still celebrating change!" I took the stairs, and as I opened the door to walk into the office, reminded myself that not everyone was going to be celebrating, and tried to contain my smile. I sat at my desk, and Rachel, on the other side of me whispered, "Cate, is that you?"

Smile containment gone. "Yes." I answered.

"Want to go smoke? I mean I know you just got here, but…"

"Sure. Give me a few minutes to check my email."

As I started up my computer my phone rang. It was Barbara, my bitch of a boss.

"Good morning Caa-aate," She has a way of drawling out my name that's so whiney. "Can you come down to my office for a few minutes?"

"I'll be right there." I hung up and reminded myself that I only had a week left to put up with her shit. Barbara has hated me since the day I started. My boss from my last job is her boss. He recruited me here, and perhaps initially she resented not having a choice about hiring me, but in time it has only gotten worse. Every proposal of mine that she reviewed has been ripped to shreds, and every idea I have voiced in a meeting has been met with a look that I call her 'Dirty Diaper Face', a look of disgust most people can only muster if they actually smell shit.

When I walked into her office, Barbara eyed me up and down, her standard greeting, evaluating one's outfit. She motioned for me to sit, and moved the box of Kleenex on her desk closer to my chair. "How are you?"

"I'm good. Surprised obviously, but good." I managed a weak smile.

"Well I just wanted you to know that I had no idea that was going to happen. They got all the directors together late yesterday morning and told us that people were getting laid off. If I had gotten a say in this, I would have fought to keep you here. I shed a lot of tears last night."

My annoyance waned. Barbara was human after all. "Thank you. It is what it is, and everything happens for a reason." I shrugged.

"If I can do anything, and I mean anything, to help you, just let me know. I can write letters of reference, whatever you need."

"I really appreciate that."

"It's just such a shock..." Her voice trailed as she twisted a Kleenex in her hand that was starting to fall apart. "I emailed you the project documentation form that they're asking everyone to complete. Let's meet this afternoon and map out next week."

"Ok. Do you know who's going to take over my account?"

Barbara sighed. "Well since Ashton & Steel is such a big client, and their program is so involved, there isn't enough time to get someone else up to speed. I'm going to take it for now, since I'm already in the loop."

"That definitely makes it easier for me. I figured I'd have to start at the beginning, training another manager."

Barbara shook her head. "No, that would be too much. This just makes sense, especially since I've already met them. They're one of our biggest accounts, and we need to minimize the impact our internal restructuring has on our clients. I just wanted to talk to you face to face this morning and tell you personally and professionally how sorry I am."

"I really appreciate that. I'll get started on the project documentation and see you this afternoon."

When I got back to my desk, I checked my email. There wasn't anything pressing. A minute later Rachel popped into my adjacent cube, cigarettes in hand. "You ready?" she asked.

"Let's do it." I said, unintentionally sounding like Tone Loc at the beginning of "Wild Thing."

When we got outside, I gave her the recap on the 'your position has been eliminated' meeting. I'm sure we weren't supposed to tell anyone the terms of our separation, but I trust Rachel. I'm really good about knowing who you can trust. I can tell you from looking at someone fifteen feet away if they would: try to steal your job, flirt with your boyfriend if you wouldn't find out, or talk trash about you when you're not around. This skill was developed in my early twenties, out of necessity after choosing more than a few really bad friends. I swear it's like a sixth sense now.

"Two weeks' severance? That's all you got? Don't they know that you left a job at Headlines to come here?" Rachel asked.

"Yeah, but they said it's strictly on how long you were here, and I'm just at a year."

"Cate, I'm sorry. That's not right."

"I'm really ok though. I'm kind of excited. This wasn't the job for me."

Rachel didn't look convinced. "Could you go back to Headlines?"

"I doubt it. They were making budget cuts when I left, and they weren't all that pleased when I came here. Besides, that wasn't the job for me either. If it had been, I wouldn't have left."

She nodded. "What are you going to do?"

"I don't know…something else. Ever since I started working on Ashton & Steel, I guess it's the subliminal marketing, but I feel like I've officially sold my soul to the devil. Worse than that, I was cheap."

"You're good at your job. You shouldn't feel bad about that."

"You can say that because your job has a real function. You're a graphic designer. Your work is tangible. You'd feel differently if you were secretly embedding images into your work. When I first started out, I was helping mom and pop businesses draw in customers. It barely paid the bills, but I felt good about it, you know? How the hell I ended up scheming with a retail giant is beyond me."

"Girl, you gotta give yourself a break. I hear what you're saying, but companies like that are going to do what they're going to do. If you aren't doing that job, somebody else will."

"I know, but I don't even want to be a piece of that puzzle anymore. I don't think I'm going to change the world or anything…unless I go on Oprah and tell their dirty secrets."

Rachel laughed. "Have you lost your fuckin' mind? Barbara would bbq your ass on a stick if she heard you say that!"

"Oh please, Barbara isn't coming near the smoke hole. If she didn't go around the front parking lot she couldn't work her "Jag" into a conversation every day…"

I breezed through the rest of my work day and even got through my meeting with Barbara without the usual tension. For the first time ever, Barbara refrained from making snide comments about my appearance or belongings. Usually she finds one thing to disparage at the start of a meeting. Like the time I brought in my new Kate Spade tote, which I had thought was perfect since my laptop fit in it, and it worked simultaneously as a purse. As soon as I walked into the conference room that day, Barbara had to say what an interesting "satchel" it was; emphasizing the word "satchel" like it was synonymous with trash bag. Then she went on and on about who would have thought to put a laptop in it, saying that most people would have thought of it as more of a diaper bag. I hated that I could never predict what part of me she would pick apart on any given day, leaving me too surprised to come up with any retort that would let me maintain some dignity. Instead I was always sitting there, with a feeble smiling deer in the headlights look, as I tried to change the subject from whatever she had honed in on.

Today was different. We went through the details of Ashton & Steel's program without a single snarky comment. Barbara probably assumed I was devastated about losing my job, and it was less fun to kick me when I was that far down, but I decided to accept it as a gift. Maybe my last week at this job would be better than the last year.

When I left the office I resisted the urge to go to happy hour, knowing that I had to evaluate my finances and options for the future. Besides, there would be plenty of time for happy hours, which would no longer be filled with me bitching about my job. I just had to find my new direction.

I went home and started assessing my situation. I had saved enough to support myself for five months. It wasn't enough to support my usual spending habits, but I could pare down. After all, my choices had only gotten fancy in the last year. Obviously I didn't need the $48 Laura Mercier body scrub. I could switch to the $16 scrub at Bath & Body Works and cut back by two-thirds. This was going to be easy. I survived on a third of my current salary when I started my career, and I could do it again, especially since that seemed the amount my spending had increased. I could go through the cosmetic gifts with purchase that were sitting in my closet, instead of buying new products. I probably had enough samples to last six months.

I didn't need to buy olive oil, spices and hand soap from Williams & Sonoma. The grocery store brands would do fine. I didn't need to go out for drinks. I could invite friends over for drinks at my place, eliminating the enormous markup at restaurants and bars. I should thank my lucky stars I watched Suze Orman on Oprah last year, or I wouldn't have nearly as much saved.

Suze also talked about how to reduce your expenses. I'm sure she would die if she knew what I spend on my hair cuts and highlights, let alone styling products. At least I already make my own coffee at home, instead of spending fifteen bucks a week at Starbucks. I made a list of things I could cut back on. TiVo is a necessity, but I could go without HBO and Showtime. I obviously shouldn't try to cut my own hair, and after the 'orange incident', I should leave highlights to the professionals too. But I could start doing my own manicures and pedicures. I could probably do my own bikini waxes too with a kit from the store. It can't be that hard and now I'll have more time. I'll do yoga and the added flexibility will make it easier.

Evaluating my situation had only taken an hour. I had even made budget cuts! I was taking charge.

If only James, cheating sack of shit that he is, could see me now. Not even two hours after I walked in on him having sex with his boss, he scurried over to my place saying that he couldn't help himself because he'd been seduced and overpowered by her 'take charge attitude'. For the life of me, I still don't know who he thought he was dealing with. I took charge that minute by throwing every piece of clothing he had in a drawer in my condo off the balcony. I also took charge of calling the hotel we had booked for our wedding reception, explaining our *situation* to the kind coordinator and having her send me back the deposit he paid on his credit card.

For months after, I thought I would hate him as soon as the hurt was gone, but despite the occasional flashes of anger, now I mainly remember what it was like when it was good between us. It makes me sick that sometimes I still miss him. Since it's too pathetic to admit, I don't tell anyone. Especially since I would tell Jill and Kay, and unlike me, they both hate him now. So whenever this nostalgic feeling comes over me, I either force myself to picture how his boss's legs were hanging over his shoulders when I walked in, or go out for drinks. Lately I have scarily numbed to the image, so the cocktail usually wins.

Justifying that it had only been a day since I got laid off and an hour since I came up with a financial plan, I decided that I could go out for drinks. After all, you don't have to put a plan into action the second you come up with it. I called Kay and met her at her favorite new place, a wine bar which has a big deck with heat lamps where we can smoke. I love my sister for a million different reasons, but it's always enough that without fail, seeing her face makes me feel better.

She was already on the deck when I got there. With blonde hair, blue eyes and at least three inches of height on me, most people wouldn't believe we're sisters if we didn't have the same facial bone structure. "You got here fast!" she said as she leaned over to hug me. "I ordered a bottle of merlot."

There's nothing like arriving to an open bottle of Prosperity Merlot, and a big glass with your name on it. "Good choice! Here's to prosperity, the wine and my hope for the future!"

"How did it go today? Before I forget, Mom called today to see how you were taking the news. I told her you were celebrating change..."

"Ok, I'll call her tomorrow." Kay and I both knew I wouldn't. Mom would put me in full panic, especially if I told her how little I had in savings. "Today was fine, but what you'd expect. The office was quite somber. I'm certain I was the only person who was celebrating last night. Even Barbara was different; she was kind of nice today."

"What do you mean nice?" Kay was squinting skeptically, which is undoubtedly a catalyst for crow's feet in my opinion.

"Well she didn't say anything nasty which is a small miracle, and even told me how sorry she was that I got laid off."

"Huh." I know Kay's 'huh' very well. That's what she says when she thinks she knows something I don't. Not wanting to dampen my mood, I chose to ignore it.

"I don't know how long she could possibly stay on good behavior, but I just have to get through the rest of the week."

"And after that? Have you given any thought to what you want to do?"

"Yeah" I stalled for time by filling my glass. "I think I want to start my own business or something."

"Marketing?"

"No, I'm done with that. I don't want to go back to advertising either. You know Tom Robbins, the guy who wrote Jitterbug Perfume?" Kay nodded. "He said, 'The more advertising I see, the less I want to buy.' That's how I feel, turned off by the whole thing. I want something completely different now. I want to feel good about how I spend my days. I want to do something I'm passionate about, something that excites me. "

"Like what?"

"I don't know yet, but you know that bread shop in Buckhead on the corner of Piedmont? Whenever I go in there, the owner is smiling behind the counter. She remembers my name, and you can tell that she's genuinely happy. There's classical music in the background…I swear every time I walk in there I feel myself relax."

"That's because you love bread." Kay laughed. It's true, I do love bread.

"It's more than that. It's like the place is filled with happiness."

"Maybe it is," Kay said. "Like the casinos that have oxygen pumped into the air."

"I'm serious. I think that woman is living her dream, and you can feel it. My dream will come to me, like the change of course I prayed for before getting laid off."

"Good for you! Cate, I know whatever you decide to do will be great."

As we finished our wine and talked about nothing and everything, I couldn't help but think about how blessed I am. There are people who are told their entire lives that they can't do things. Yet here I am, with a sister who has always told me that I can do whatever I set my mind to, and I believe her.

CHAPTER 3

Dear Oprah,

I saw the most ridiculous thing on the cover of a tabloid today, a headline saying that you and Gayle are secret lovers. I'm sure with your strong character; you would never let that kind of nonsense bother you. What shocked me was that the person who wrote the article, if you can even classify it as such, is a woman! I feel sorry for her because she has obviously never had a real girl friend if she can't understand your relationship with Gayle without trying to make it romantic. This woman needs some real friends!

I've relied on my friends to get me through the rough times and share the good times. It's like when you said, "Lots of people want to ride with you in the limo, but what you want is someone who will take the bus with you when the limo breaks down." My best friend Jill is a bus friend. She was on a business trip in Ohio when my fiancé and I broke up. A storm was starting there and she couldn't get a flight out, so she rented a car and drove home just to be there for me. When my grandmother died, she held my hand through the funeral. Years ago I won a cruise for two to the Bahamas. I took Jill because the one thing I'm sure of, the men in our lives seem to come and go, and here we remain, together as dear friends. You don't talk much about your relationship with Stedman anymore, which I think is smart, but I'm sure you know that whatever happens with him, Gayle will be there. Anyone who doesn't get that is an idiot.

Regards,

Cate

P.S. If you and Gayle were a couple, I would totally support your relationship. I'm just saying, I know you're not.

Somehow I made it to my last day at the office. It went by faster than I'd expected. I guess when you know there's an end in sight, time picks up the pace. It helps that my outlook has changed. This is the first time I've felt like I'm on the right path, like I'm exactly where I'm supposed to be in my life. It also doesn't hurt that Barbara has been nice all week. I haven't had to listen to one comment about how "unusual" my wardrobe choices are, which is hard to stomach when they're coming from someone who shops at Talbots.

Rachel popped into my cube shortly after I got in the office. We're supposed to call them work spaces, because upper management, people with offices, thinks that sounds better, but I like to call things what they are. My workspace is a cubicle without a window. You could call it an executive suite, but that wouldn't change anything about it. "Want to go smoke?" She asked.

"Yes, please!"

As soon as we got outside, curiosity got the best of me. "So what's the word around the office?" I'd been so busy getting the Ashton & Steel account ready for my departure that I had been out of the loop on all the gossip.

Rachel took a deep drag. "Consensus is that there are probably more layoffs to come. Everyone who didn't get laid off is pissed because their work load is almost doubling, without a chance of a raise. Yet they still have to act like they're grateful to have a job while waiting to see if they actually do. Everyone who was laid off has been pretty quiet about it, except Justin. You know he's been here for eight years. He's caught up in the 'why me' thing."

"What's the point? The decisions were made by people in another state. They probably just looked at standard factors: salaries, client base, and tenure, whatever..."

"Apparently it was more than that. Each director picked the people on their team they wanted to get rid of."

"What? How do you know that?"

"I heard Barbara and Janet talking."

"Barbara told me that she would have fought for my job, but didn't have a say."

"I don't know what to tell ya, Cate. Barbara lied."

"Why would she lie? She didn't have to say anything!"

"Because she's a conniving bitch. You know that."

"What exactly did you hear?"

"They were in Janet's office. I guess they thought everyone was gone, because the door was open. Janet said that she was glad that they got to choose and that there wouldn't be dead weight on her team anymore."

"What did Barbara say?" I was still trying to wrap my mind around it.

"I don't remember her exact words, but she definitely agreed."

"Rachel, tell me what she said. I want to know." Rachel eyed me, like she was trying to choose her words. "Just tell me."

"Barbara said she was glad that she wouldn't have to put up with any more of your shit."

"I'm smoking another one." I said as I got my cigarettes out of my coat pocket.

"Me too. Can I bum one?" I handed her a cigarette. "I'm sorry. I shouldn't have told you."

"No, I'm glad you did." We stood there puffing away in silence. I couldn't believe I fell for her load of bullshit. I knew better! My new found zen feeling was wearing off wicked fast, and anger was taking its place with such speed that my face was reddening.

"Fuck her. You know Cate, you could get a job anywhere. I did want to ask you though, what happened with that presentation you were working on? You know the proposal you had me proof for typos on sensory selling?"

"That was last week. Of course I know the one. I lost my job, not my memory...Sorry, I'm just pissed. Barbara shit all over it. She said my analysis was weak, that I took too many liberties interpreting the data."

"When I left last night, Barbara was in the conference room, presenting it to the sales team."

"What? Are you sure? You've got to be kidding me."

"I'm positive."

"I can't believe she did that. I hate this! I feel like I'm getting duped and don't even know how or why. And worse, there's nothing I can do."

"I'm sorry, Cate. I debated whether or not to tell you, since I knew it would just piss you off, but I thought you had a right to know. I'd want to know if I were you."

"Thanks Rachel. Seriously, I appreciate it."

"Are you going to say anything to her?"

"I would love to say something to her. Hell, I'd love to say all sorts of shit to her, like tell her that no matter how many times that she says she's a size two, she's not. That her "Jag" doesn't make her classy, and that everyone can hear her fighting with her husband on the phone every freakin' day."

Rachel laughed. "I like it. Kitty's got claws!"

"Barbara is a stupid twat, but that doesn't change who I am. I can still take the high road. I definitely won't run into her there."

"Cate, you are good people. What am I going to do without you here? Who's going to tell me what happened on Oprah?"

"TiVo, Rachel, I'm telling you, you have to get it. Email me, meet me for drinks. You'll be fine."

"Do me a favor. Find a job somewhere great and take me with you!"

I took a long lunch, and the rest of the day went by quickly. I had been taking a few things from my desk home every day, so there wasn't anything left to pack up. I had a bullshit meeting with Barbara late afternoon, to wrap up any loose ends. I left quietly afterwards, avoiding goodbyes.

Jill was meeting me at the pub after work to celebrate my last day. She wasn't there when I arrived, so I went inside and snagged two seats at the bar. I ordered a dirty martini and started thinking about the Dr. Seuss book *Oh, the Places You'll Go* that Kay gave me when I graduated from high school. This would be just like that. I could do whatever I wanted, as soon as I figured out what that was.

I was trying to picture what I would look like as a cartoon character when Jill sat down. "Congratulations! You made it through your last day! So how was it?"

"I don't know what to call it, but I'm glad it's over. I found out that Barbara did have a say in who was let go, and on top of that, the stupid bitch started taking credit for my work before I was even out the door!"

"Oh my God! How did you find that out?"

"Rachel told me. Then at the end of the day Barbara tried to pretend she was all torn up about seeing me go, like I don't know that she hates me. She must have been upset about something else, because she managed to squeeze out a few crocodile tears when she was saying good bye."

Jill pushed her hair behind her ears, a habit she developed when she started growing out her bob last year. "Well, what did you expect?"

"I don't know…but it never occurred to me that she would fake tears. I thought we were done when she asked again if there was anything she could do, and I stunned her by saying that a recommendation on my LinkedIn profile would be great."

"Good for you! Do you think she will?"

"Yeah, she already did it. I'm sure she felt like she had to because I went back to my desk and immediately sent her the request. Then I walked back to her office, told her that I knew she was busy, but I needed her to do it right then. I said I was applying for a job that required one more recommendation before it would let me submit my resume, and that I had to do it today."

"Were you?"

"Nope, but I figured that since I endured her bullshit this entire week, the least she could do was live up to her offer. And I needed it since I don't think I would get a recommendation out of her now that I'm gone."

"Nice. Seriously, well done. Imagine how this past year would have gone if you'd started playing her game sooner."

"That's the thing. I don't want to play her game. I don't want to play the corporate game anymore either. It doesn't come naturally to me. I don't know how you do it."

"It doesn't get to me like it gets to you. For me it's like a chess game. You just watch the moves, the strategy, and play back."

"That's exhausting to me. I hate how everybody's fake, and I never know what to do anyway. I don't have the instincts for it."

"If you didn't have the instincts for it, you wouldn't have made it this far."

"Nah, I just survived. I would have been further up the ladder if I understood the rules. Remember at Headlines when I got passed up for that promotion before I left? That probably happened a few times, and I didn't even realize it. I was too honest. I thought that when they asked for my opinion, they wanted to know. Really they just wanted to have their egos massaged and if you're the schmuck telling them what you really think instead of what they want to hear, you're never going to get ahead. I've been that schmuck from the beginning."

"So now what?"

"Now I just have to find my place, where I fit in."

"You know if you change your mind, I can see what they have at my company."

"I'm not changing my mind. It was a sign, remember?"

"Ah, yes." Jill said, clearly humoring me. "Have you gotten any other signs?"

"No, but I've got some ideas."

"Like what?"

"There are so many possibilities; I don't know where to start. I want to do something that makes me happy. Do you know that most heart attacks happen between eight and nine a.m. on Mondays?"

"No, but I'll be sure to keep that in mind when we play trivia."

"It's true. So first things first, I need to choose something that won't induce a heart attack. I can rule out anything that would require going back to school. Maybe I could be a nose!"

"A what?"

"A nose, you know the people who make fragrances? I love perfume. I would be great at that. I appreciate the significance of things olfactory. Like how someone can die and years later when you're memory won't conjure up their face clearly or you can't hear their voice anymore, you can smell the fragrance you associate with them, and boom! It's almost overwhelming; they come back to your mind so fast. Every time I smell some combination of baked apples and ginger, I immediately remember my great aunt Eugenia and she died a long time ago. Maybe I could make that, call it the 'Signature Genia Scent'.

I could open a candle store, featuring the scents I created! Or a cheese shop. I love cheese! There are probably tons of jobs that I've never even heard of that I would love. I could be a food critic. I love food and have a lot of opinions about it.

Or instead of a cheese shop, I could make my own blue cheese dressing. I love blue cheese dressing. It's my favorite condiment, perfect on salad, also on anything with potatoes. Whenever I'm at Publix I always look to see if there's a new one, since the bottled ones I've tried aren't great. Maybe I could make the best blue cheese dressing, and sell it to all the fine dining restaurants in town. Then when there's a high demand for it, I could bottle it and sell it at grocery stores!"

Jill put her head in her hands. "What? Um, have you given this a lot of thought?" Jill looked up, laughing.

"Kind of. Well, while I was waiting for you to get here." I admitted. "Why?"

"Oh, just wondering. Sounds like you've got your work cut out for you, a lot of research in your future. I would say the world's your oyster, but I'd hate to encourage some weird ass oyster farming experiment, since you love them too."

"No worries, too stinky."

"Too stinky? What do you think the cheese thing would smell like?"

"I don't know. I hadn't thought about that, but I'm at the formative stage now. Anyway, enough about me. Catch me up, what's new with you?"

Jill shrugged and looked away. "Nothing really." This is how things have been for the past year. She met Steven at a work conference and has been dating him ever since, even after he fessed up to being married. At first she told me about how unhappily married he is, and his top three reasons why he can't simply leave his wife, all of which are merely ridiculous excuses from some standard 'men who cheat on their wives' handbook. Initially I listened with the same begrudging tolerance that Jill extends towards my smoking. Then as it grew more serious, and seedier if that's even possible, I got to where it was too much to hear without constantly putting my two cents in. For months she talked about how she needed to end it, but was seeing him more frequently. I got her a book about women who date married men, why they do it and how to heal, which I don't think she read.

The night I caught James cheating on me, I ranted and raved to Jill, calling the other woman a horrible cow, a miserable pathetic bitch who at best could only fuck someone else's man. Since then, she hasn't talked about her relationship. Outside of our shared activities, which usually are more than enough to talk about, she only talks about work and her family. I hate that there's such a big part of her life that she can't talk to me about, almost as much as I hate that she's dating him.

CHAPTER 4

Dear Oprah,

I don't have any religious affiliation, much less authority of any nature, but I would still like to nominate you as Saint of All Things Possible. I am at a turning point in my life, and feel inspired by you that everything is possible for me. Even when I'm watching your show, sometimes I'm overwhelmed thinking about how far you've come: born into poverty in rural Mississippi and the profound hardships that you endured in your upbringing.

I am so proud of you; you would think that I participated in your development somehow. Although I have been an avid fan forever, I obviously didn't contribute to what has made you the phenomenal woman you are today. You are the person I admire most. You turned your program from a talk show, to something that makes people better whether by reading, fitness, spiritual development, or financial guidance. So I guess you could say that you have contributed to my development. I hope I can become somebody who does something great and meaningful, so that you would have reason to be proud of me too.

Regards,

Cate

P.S. If anything comes about with the sainthood thing, I'll let you know immediately.

I decided that to start a new life, I needed to start with a clean slate, a clean condo to bring clarity to my thoughts and a sanitary place to start making my own blue cheese dressing. Now I'm wishing that I had hired someone to clean it thoroughly, just once before I lost my job. Since I can't turn back the clock, and I certainly can't justify paying someone now, I rolled up my sleeves and went to work. I'm embarrassed to say that my place was filthy. It looked fine until I started moving things around. I don't know what the hell constitutes a dust bunny, but I hope there aren't any living organisms involved. Although I did find almost two dollars worth of change under the couch cushions, I also found a few old pretzels, a bunch of pony tail holders, and a fingernail file. It was disgusting. I swiffered the floors and vacuumed the rugs. Now I know why my white socks turn brown on the bottom. I scrubbed every inch of my kitchen, even cleaning the oven and the refrigerator. My place is so small I can't believe that it took ten hours, but it was worth it.

It feels invigorating to have a clean home, and a kitchen worthy of Cate's Blue Cheese Dressing! I decided to leave salad off of the label so people will quit thinking of it as something you put on salad, and start using it as the versatile condiment it is. I bought the best blue cheese you can find, Maytag, shipped all the way from Iowa. It was expensive, but it will pay off since you need the best ingredients to make the best product. Since I don't have a lot of money for start up expenses, I bought it in bulk to save on shipping.

The first batch came out tangy and watery, undoubtedly from too much vinegar. I stirred more blue cheese in, which resulted in something akin to clumpy soup. After wasting more of my fancy blue cheese trying to fix it, I had to dump it out and start over. The next batch was still too tangy, bordering on acidic. I figured that I needed to upgrade my key ingredients, so I went to Whole Foods and bought organic buttermilk, a variety of mustards and four different kinds of vinegar. Even though the expenditures were adding up, when I got the right formula, I could make different varieties of my dressing and expand my market.

Five hours and seven batches later, my kitchen is a disaster area. The first two attempts went into my garbage disposal, which is now completely backed up into my sink like a nasty milky swamp with clumps of brown lettuce that must have been stuck in there from the night before. The mixing bowls were too big for the dish washer, and I couldn't float them in the swamp sink. Since every surface in my tiny kitchen is occupied by a variety of ingredients, the bowls are on the table in what doubles as my living and dining room.

I realized that my other investment, my newly acquired Kitchen Aid Mixer was not the right tool for the job, and decided to try my blender. I finally got one batch that had both consistency and color resembling blue cheese dressing, but needed a stronger flavor. I was adding more blue cheese, using the hole in the lid to pour it in. The blender must have been too full. It spewed like a volcano erupting with whitish gray slime all over me and what had started the day as my clean work space. Startled, I jumped back and knocked over the open carton of buttermilk which instantly coated the floor.

I gave myself a pep talk. *I am not one to be defeated! You cannot cry over spilled blue cheese. You will not give up. What would Oprah do?*

My mind didn't want to participate...*Oprah would hire someone to clean this shit up!*

In a battle of wills with myself, I was determined to stay focused, *No, she got to where she is today by cleaning up her own messes. Look at where she is today. Oprah would not stand here staring at this mess, she would jump into action! You can do this!*

I grabbed a roll of paper towels, only to discover that blue cheese was all over it. There was no use spreading more of it around, so I walked to my linen closet to get a fresh roll. My kitchen had started out pristine and with elbow grease and Spic & Span, it would be clean again.

After I soaked up most of the buttermilk from the floor, I started wiping off the blue cheese gunk from the countertops. With the consistency of glue, it was smearing everywhere. After I got the first layer off, I could see the black granite counter beneath it. I wiped off the stove top and the front of the refrigerator, but I could see white trails dripping further back than I could reach. I took the swiffer figuring I could use it to get between the refrigerator and the wall. As I stretched, almost reaching the back, my feet slid out from under me. I fell to the floor, pain shooting through my ankle. It hurt to move, but I had lost my will to get up anyway. I sat on the floor, trying not to cry. I started to give myself another pep talk when I felt something land on my head, like bird shit. I touched it, blue cheese in my hair. Then another clump hit my nose. I looked up and saw the veiny blue from the cheese throughout my textured ceiling pattern. It hadn't occurred to me that it had erupted all the way to the ceiling. As I sat there with my ankle throbbing, it dripped on the countertop I had just scrubbed. I couldn't hold back my tears.

There was a knock at the door. I couldn't be bothered to get up so I yelled. "Who is it?"

"It's me. Open up." Kay's voice came through the door.

"Can't. Use your key." I listened to Kay rummage through her purse for what seemed like an eternity before the door opened.

"Oh my God, Cate, what the fuck happened? Why are you on the floor?"

"I twisted my ankle. What are you doing here?"

Kay held up a bottle of champagne, as she looked around the room. "Remember, we were going to celebrate your first day as a blue cheese dressing maker?

"Oh yeah, I forgot."

"You can't get up?" She asked, looking more confused than concerned.

"I probably can…haven't tried."

"Holy shit! What is that smell?" She stared at the ceiling. Apparently she's faster at surveying a mess than I am.

"It's holy shit, Kay. I have ordained feces in here."

"Seriously, is that the blue cheese?" She put down the champagne and held her nose like that was going to help.

"Seems so. I guess I got used to it."

"Alright, get your ass up and tell me what happened. I'll help you clean."

I burst into tears. Sometimes things are so bad that just having someone be nice to you makes you crumble faster than the finest blue cheese. "Don't come in here," I blubbered, "you'll get it all over your work clothes."

Kay walked over anyway and extended her hand. "Come on; see if you can put some weight on it." I took her hand, and stood up. "See, things are already getting better, you're off the floor. Now let's start cleaning this shit up."

We swiffered the ceiling, which to my surprise actually worked, and wiped everything down. While we scrubbed, I told her about my disaster of a day. It went so much faster with two people, in no time we were done and ready for champagne.

Kay uncorked the bottle. "Let's take this out on the patio. At least your place can air out while we drink."

I grabbed the glasses. "Thanks, Kay. I'm sure this isn't how you wanted to spend your evening."

"Sure it is. We planned on champagne, and now we're drinking it."

"I don't know what I'd do without you. You know, I waited all week to get the blue cheese, and now I have wasted more than a pound of it spraying it all over the kitchen."

"It wasn't a total waste. You learned something, right?"

"Yeah, I learned there's more to making blue cheese dressing than I ever thought."

"It's a start. How are you going to be the next Mrs. Dash if you don't start somewhere?"

I sipped the last of the champagne from my glass. "Why does champagne always go so fast? We've already gone through more than half of this bottle."

"Because it's the nectar of the Gods. When you make it big, you have got to stock the fridge with it." Kay held out her glass. "Fill 'er up!"

"I don't see that happening anytime soon."

"Cate Sanders, you had a bad day. That's it. Remember Grandpa always said, 'If you want to ride, you've got to stay on the horse', so chin up and keep going. Other than the mess, how did it taste?"

"I don't know. I think it was getting better toward the end, but my taste buds are overloaded now."

"Want me to try it? Now that it's not permeating my nostrils, I could tell you."

The bubbly had brought my spirits back from the muck, so I jumped at the chance. I ran inside and got a plate together, with celery and the sweet potato wedges I'd baked. On the side, I put the small amount of dressing that had survived the blender fiasco and hurried back to the patio. "Now remember this is my first attempt." I said as I placed it in front of her. Kay took a bite. I knew it couldn't be too terrible since she didn't spit it out.

"Cate, this is so good! Seriously, I wouldn't change a thing."

If I hadn't been sitting down, I would have fallen over from the shock. "Really? You think so? You don't think it's too tangy or anything?"

"I swear to God, this is the best blue cheese dressing I have ever tasted. It's creamy, and the crumbles are the perfect size. There is a nice little crunch or something to it."

"Oh my God, I can't believe it! It's my secret ingredient, seeds from one of the mustards!"

"It works! Look at that, you did it on your first day!"

I was shocked. I had come up with my recipe, just like that. After Kay left, I was too wound up to sleep so I started working on my business plan. All I had to do was sell it to a nice restaurant, something upscale. Remembering that Jill's neighbor Thomas owns a posh restaurant downtown, I decided to have a tasting party and get Jill to invite him. I would invite all of my old advertising contacts too. Surely somebody would be interested.

The next morning I started making the arrangements. Since my condo is so small, I asked Jill if I could use her house, which was brilliant since it would also make it easier to get her neighbor restaurateur there. Everything fell into place. My debut tasting party would be next week.

I went straight to work making small batches, careful to avoid another blender incident. My menu was simple but varied: rosemary crostinis and small new potatoes with my dressing baked on top, gourmet olives stuffed with dressing, and sweet potato wedges and vegetable trays for sampling it as a cold dip. The definitive presentation was small iceberg wedge salads with perfect dollops of dressing on top, barely running over the sides. I quickly realized that I had to quit sampling my creations if I wanted to fit into anything I owned for the big night. That was a good thing since there wasn't any extra room when I put on my favorite black dress pants.

Kay met me at Jill's place late that afternoon, so we could get everything ready. She walked in carrying a stack of big stainless tubs. "Where'd you get those?"

"They're on loan from Lainey. We figured you needed something to keep the white wine chilled in." Lainey is Kay's best friend. They were roommates in college and before she got married a few years ago, she was practically the third Sanders sister. She married a big football sportscaster, quit her job and started traveling around with him. Now we hardly ever see her.

"Does that mean Lainey's coming?"

Before Kay could answer, Lainey walked up behind her. If it weren't for her big hair, I wouldn't have known who it was behind the stainless tub until I heard her deep southern accent, "Dahlin', I wouldn't miss this for the world! Now where can I put this hooch, so I can give your little ass a hug?"

I took the case from her and yelled, "Jill! Come out here, you'll never believe who it is!"

Everything was perfect. With Jill, Lainey and Kay, I had all my girls together for the first time since the 4th of July.

While I put the food together on serving trays, Lainey and Jill filled the bins with ice and white wine. Kay put out the fresh bouquets of flowers and tea light candles. "Ok, I'm not lighting the candles until right before go time, so other than that you can consider it decorated. How's it going in there?" Kay asked me.

"I'm pretty much done too." I answered. "Everything baked is on the heated serving trays. Everything chilled is in the fridge on the crystal platters. The red wine is on the buffet, so I think we're all set."

Kay walked into the kitchen, and started eyeing a little plate on the counter with a sampling of every item on my menu. "What's this?"

"That is a sampler platter for y'all. Go ahead, there's plenty. Besides, those are the ones with minor imperfections and I want everything to look just right!"

"You don't have to tell me twice," Kay said before popping an olive into her mouth. Lainey walked over and ate one too.

"Oh my God, these are delicious! Kay said they were good, but this is like a little piece of heaven. Where's Jill? She better get in here before we eat all of the olives."

"Jill doesn't like blue cheese." I said. "She only likes her cheese yellow and individually wrapped in plastic."

"What do I like wrapped in plastic?" Jill asked as she emerged from the bathroom.

"Big dicks." Kay answered as she dipped one of the sweet potato wedges in blue cheese dressing.

"Oh please, the biggest benefit when I get married someday will be saying sayonara to condoms. Seriously, what are you talking about?"

"I was telling Kay and Lainey that you're not a fan of blue cheese just that processed pasteurized crap."

"Yum, grilled cheese sandwiches. So what if I order off the kid's menu? Chicken fingers, peanut butter and jelly, that's my palate."

"It's not like it matters anyway." I said. "Jill hardly eats, so she's not exactly my target audience."

"What? I eat plenty. When I get busy, it's not that high on my priority list."

"Cate, you want in on this?" Lainey asked, holding up the last olive.

"I'm too nervous to eat, so that's all you."

Lainey shook her head. "Cate, there's no reason to be nervous. Everybody who's going to be here tonight will be here to support you."

"I don't even know some of these people. I sent the invite out to every chef I could find on a directory listing."

Kay handed me a glass of wine and said, "Cate, it's going to be great. A little pinot noir should help you relax."

Like clockwork, there was a knock on the door at eight and people streamed in for the next fifteen minutes. I couldn't believe how big the turnout was.

There were at least 60 people. Kay and Lainey got the cold platters circulating, and Jill steered people to the table with the warm trays and the wedge salads. In no time, wine glasses were filled and people were putting my creations onto their plates. It was brilliant! I mingled and tried to contain my enthusiasm as people told me how delicious everything was.

Jill introduced me to Thomas, her restaurateur neighbor, who was very complimentary. He admitted with the kind of caution you would expect if he was confessing that he robbed a bank, that he used premixed salad dressings at his restaurant. He said that he had planned on making a change and that he would love to use my dressing! I was so amazed, I hugged him. He said he'd love to try more and asked if I was going to make vinaigrettes too. Before I could answer, someone tapped me on the shoulder. As I turned, my grin quickly faded. It was Barbara.

"Caa-aate, how are you?" She gave me the kind of hug where you hardly touch the other person except to pat them on the back. The irony of her patting me on the back was not lost on me as I wondered if there was now a knife protruding from mine. I have never been more grateful to have Jill standing beside me.

"I'm great!" I said as I made every effort not to clench my teeth. Thomas excused himself to get more wine. "Barbara, this is my friend Jill, who was kind enough to host this party."

"You have such a lovely home." Barbara eyed Jill up and down, and it was all I could do not to bust out laughing when Jill did it right back to her without saying a word.

"I'm surprised to see you here." I said, wondering if I was the one making the diaper face now.

"My son is the chef at Alouette. When he told me about this little get together, I couldn't believe the coincidence. I figured I'd tag along and see how you're holding up."

I stood there speechless, unable to believe the bitch was still getting under my skin. Jill came to the rescue. "I'd say she's doing more than holding up. She's already well on her way to starting her own business. This *little get together* is just the beginning."

Jill's wording wasn't lost on Barbara. "Well, I'll let you girls get back to it. I just wanted to say hello."

When I was sure she was out of ear shot I said, "I can't believe she is here. Seriously Jill, what the hell?"

"You're fine. Don't let her get to you. This is one night, and it's your night. I'm here. You've got Lainey and Kay here too, so the three of us we can keep her out of your way. You need to relax and keep mingling."

I surveyed the room. "I don't see Kay or Lainey. Do you think they ducked out back to smoke?"

"I doubt it, but why don't you go look and take a few deep breaths? And Cate, if they're smoking, don't you dare join them. It's already nine thirty. Since it's a week night, people will probably clear out of here soon. You need to work the room and smelling like an ashtray isn't going to get you business."

I went to the back deck, expecting to see the tell tale red glow of lit cigarette tips, but they weren't there. I looked everywhere until the only place I hadn't checked was Jill's bedroom. It wasn't like them to desert me. As I opened the door to Jill's bedroom, I heard the unmistakable sound of vomiting. I walked over to her bathroom, and there they were. Lainey was kneeling in front of the toilet, and Kay was hanging on to the side of the bath tub. "Oh, no! What's going on?"

Kay projectile vomited into the bath tub. Lainey lifted her head up just enough to meet my eyes. There was a trail of vomit coming from one corner of her mouth. "Honey, I think your blue cheese was the victim of some serious bacteria."

"That can't be! I just got it last week! It's made from bacteria." Lainey put her head back down on the rim of the toilet bowl, which was also covered in vomit. "Oh fuck! Fuck, fuck, fuck." I grabbed some wash cloths from Jill's closet, ran cold water over them and tried to wipe the vomit off Lainey's face. Another wave came over her, and she threw up again, missing the toilet entirely.

There was a low mumble coming from the bathtub. "Get Jill" Kay groaned.

Panic stricken, I ran back to the living room. Jill was nodding and smiling to one of the guests. I caught her eye, and she waved me over. "Cate, this is Sean from Aria. Sean, this is Cate, the woman behind the blue cheese." He put his hand out, and I shook it. It wasn't until I saw Jill and Sean staring at my hand like I was a leper that I realized I was still holding the wash cloth, which was covered in vomit.

"Oh shit! I'm so sorry. Shit! Did I get it on your hand?"

"Yes, you did. What the hell is it?"

Jill grabbed a cocktail napkin from the table and handed it to him.

Sean stared at his palm. "Is this vomit?" He practically yelled, and the room got so quiet you could have heard a pen drop. Instead there was only the sound of Kay and Lainey retching, which might as well have been choreographed with the sound of another guest throwing up into the kitchen sink.

The woman at the kitchen sink looked up and said, "I'm sorry. Someone was in the other bathroom. I couldn't make it outside." Then there was the sound of heaving coming from the hall bathroom too, followed by the sound of everyone else's keys jingling as they began a mass exodus.

I wanted to die, or at least hide in Jill's bedroom, but I stood there and apologized profusely to the few people who hadn't made it out the door yet. There wasn't a single friendly face. They gave each other sympathetic looks, but they were all glaring at me. As luck would have it, Barbara was still in the room. For the first time, she had an actual reason to make her diaper face, which was in full effect. Of course she couldn't just leave, she had to say something. "Well I'm glad I didn't eat anything. You've certainly outdone yourself this time." I stared at my toes and blinked hard, wishing that I was Samantha from Bewitched; that I could open my eyes and everything would be magically fixed.

When I opened my eyes, the only person left in the room was Thomas. "Listen, I don't want to be a dick, and I think this goes without saying, but I'm going to need to cancel that order." I nodded and bit my lip, trying to keep the tears from streaming down my face. He turned and walked out the door just as the dam of my lower lids flooded over. I walked back to Jill's bedroom. Kay and Lainey were on her bed, their eyes closed. Jill was in the bathroom, spraying disinfectant around the toilet. She looked up and sighed, "Well lady, no one can see you didn't make an impression."

I cried and said, "Let me do that. This is all my fault. I can't let you clean it up."

"I got it. Already cleaned up, just spraying again to help the smell."

"Are they O.K.?" I nodded my head in Lainey and Kay's direction.

"Yeah, they're fine. I brought them ginger ale and water. They've kept that down. It's out of their systems; they probably just need to sleep it off."

"Can you sleep off food poisoning? Oh my God, I poisoned everybody." I could just picture everyone that came, bent over a toilet, literally throwing up my hope for a future.

"Well, they already put back everything they ate. I don't know. It's one of the benefits of my eating habits. The stuff I eat could probably survive for years in a bomb shelter."

"Don't get me wrong. I'm so glad that you're not sick, but if the upside is that you're the only person I haven't made violently ill tonight, my life sucks."

Jill cocked her head to the side, "Did you hear that?"

"Hear what? The sound of my life going down the shitter?"

"It's coming from the bedroom."

We looked in, and there was Kay propped up on one elbow with a goofy grin. "I said it could be worse. Your life could suck uncircumcised cock."

Lainey didn't open her eyes, but she smiled, "Or wrinkled old man cock."

Kay sat up, "Or teeny tiny 3 inch cock"

Lainey opened her eyes and giggled, clutching her stomach, "…Or crooked cock."

Kay's turn, "Or never heard of man-scaping cock."

"Are y'all feeling better, or do you just have a long list of undesirable cocks on file in your heads?"

Kay stood up slowly and said, "Or sweaty, salty cock."

Lainey said, "Cate, name some bad cock. I'm not getting off this bed until you do."

Jill handed me a glass of white wine. I hadn't realized that she left the room. "Are you hearing this shit?" I asked, incredulous that they were speaking, especially to me. Jill answered laughing, "Or can't stay hard cock."

"Cate, name some bad cock, dammit." Lainey was sitting up now.

I was completely drawing a blank. I desperately racked my brain, since the least I could do after making them sick as dogs was participate. "Pee Cock!" I yelled like I had discovered a cure for the illness I had spawned! "P-E-E Cock!"

Three voices in unison yelled "Ew!"

"That's disgusting. I'm getting up." And with that Lainey grunted and got off the bed. It was almost a miracle, like Lazarus, she rose up and walked.

CHAPTER 5

Dear Oprah,

Things aren't going so well. I still know I can make something of my life, but I'm off to a rocky start. My first business endeavor after the layoff wasn't quite what I had anticipated. I know that's part of life, you can't succeed every time, but I didn't plan on having such a colossal and public failure. I keep telling myself that it's ok, that we all fall down and get back up, that we all have things that hang over our heads. A long time ago when you admitted that you had done drugs before, it was like you needed to let go of your secret shame. At first everybody was talking about it, but now that's old irrelevant news and it seems they all forgot. I wouldn't have remembered either, except my attempt to start a business was so disastrous that someone said I must have been smoking crack. So I failed once, miserably. This doesn't mean I am destined to become a failure. I know you're network hasn't had the best ratings, but I'm sure things will pick up soon. And at some point maybe my current public humiliation will be old news too. I'm going to do my best to hold my head up high and move on, taking more than a few pointers from the woman who does it with the grace of a queen.

Regards,

Cate

P.S. How long did it take for everyone to quit talking about the drug thing?

My voicemail is full. I'm so humiliated; I can't bring myself to answer the phone. Rachel called, so word of my sickness inducing soiree has inevitably spread through my old office. Barbara probably relished relaying every minute of it. Alas, I am stuck to my couch, watching Lifetime and wishing I could stay here forever or until people forget what a loser I am, whichever comes first. Worse than that, I can't even wallow in my own misery without being acutely aware of how selfish it is, after making people I care about sick, and the embarrassment I inevitably caused Jill by doing so in her home. She kept saying that I had to quit harping on that, but it's true. I was on the verge of a fresh batch of tears, the only thing I've produced in the last week, when there was a knock at my door. *Papa John's is fast today,* I thought. I had to order pizza since I can't bring myself to open the fridge and look at blue cheese or anything associated with it, and opening the door for food delivery has been the only thing motivating me to shower.

When I opened the door I discovered that it wasn't Papa John's. Kay and Lainey walked in. "Alright Missy," Lainey announced, "You can't hide in here forever." I didn't agree, but no point in arguing so I just said "I thought you were Papa John's." as I made my way back to the couch.

Kay sat down beside me. "Look, I know you want to hole up in here, but that's not going to do you any good." I stared at the TV. Cheryl Ladd was on the screen, again. That woman must be in a hundred Lifetime movies. "So pack your bag, the three of us are going to the beach."

I thought she had to be kidding, but she wasn't. Lainey's in-laws had a condo on the beach in Destin, and we had use of it for an entire week. Despite my protests that I couldn't possibly take a vacation, since I didn't have a job to take a vacation from, they were set on it. Lainey reasoned that the three of us hadn't been on a trip together in years, and that with a free place to stay I couldn't say no. Aside from the fact that I didn't deserve an escape, I couldn't come up with any reason to stay in town either. By the time the pizza came, it was settled. After we ate I would pack a bag and we would head to the beach.

After a seven hour drive, and my promise to quit apologizing and lamenting over how blue cheese can spoil for no discernible reason, we were finally there. The condo was nice, with three enormous bedrooms; their vacation home was at least five times the size of my full time residence. It looked like it had been decorated professionally. It was so fancy; I didn't feel like I belonged there, but I wanted to.

Kay went to bed not long after we arrived. Lainey and I sat on the upper deck with a bottle of red wine. I was relaxed, listening to the sound of the ocean, with the perfect night breeze on my face. Lainey said, "This is just what we needed, a little piece of heaven."

I nodded, "I could stay here forever. Do you think your in-laws would mind if I moved in here?"

"That would be a little awkward."

"Couldn't you just say that you got them a cabana girl?"

"I doubt I'll be talking to them a whole lot after Michael and I get divorced."

"What?"

She drained her glass quickly. "Things aren't working out."

"Since when? I thought you were so happy?"

"We were, but…things just changed."

"Does Kay know?" Lainey looked at me like I'd asked if the ocean was going to still be there in the morning. "Shit Lainey, I'm so sorry. I had no idea."

"Why would you? I've been off in every direction, following Michael wherever his work takes him. All the while with a stupid ass grin on my face, faking it so well it took the last six months for me to see it for what it is."

"God Lainey, here I've been with my head so far up my own ass, I didn't even realize…" I thought about how I'd run my mouth the whole drive down, like I was the only person in the world with a problem. I'd even envied Lainey's perfect worry free life.

"You think you're the one with your head up your ass? I've been so self absorbed with trying to make my marriage work, never realizing that I was the only person trying, that I've been a shitty invisible friend to everybody. Feels like I'm the prodigal friend, crawling back with my tail between my legs."

"No, you haven't." I said, trying to put a little conviction behind the words but remembering how Kay had bitched up a storm when Lainey first started the disappearing act. "What makes you think Michael doesn't want to make it work?"

Lainey filled our quickly emptied glasses and took a long sip, "Well when he said, 'Lainey, I want a divorce' that was my big clue. I'd been pressing him to go to marriage counseling, since it felt like we had been growing apart almost since our honeymoon. Do you know that on our wedding night, he spent two hours replying to emails?"

"I don't even know what to say."

"You could start by saying what I tell myself, 'Lainey, you're a dumbass for quitting your job.' I should have known better."

"You are not a dumbass. Why is it that you are so hard on yourself, but you're so easy on everybody else? If I were in your shoes, you'd be telling me that I'm fabulous and that I made decisions in good faith with the information I had at the time. You'd say that everything was going to be fine."

Lainey looked up at the wooden beams on the ceiling of the deck, quiet for a minute. "You're right. I don't know, maybe because I saw it coming. I've had months to look back in the rear view mirror of my marriage, and let me tell ya, the signs were there. It was red flag central, but I just ignored it, carrying on like everything was fine. It's weird though, the last month or so things had gotten better. We were getting along great."

I remembered how the same thing had gone through my head; that James had been noticeably more attentive in the months before I caught him cheating on me. When I found out that he had been sleeping with his boss for a while, and the night I walked in on them hadn't been a sole indiscretion, I was baffled. "I hate to even bring this up, but do you think he's having an affair?"

"No. He's not like that. Besides, he doesn't have time for an affair, anymore than he's had the opportunity. I travel with him everywhere he goes. Travelled, I should say. I'm going to have to get used to us being past tense. Cate, I haven't worked in two years. And now, I don't even have what I started with. I've lost touch with all of my old friends, not to mention my work contacts. I don't know what I'm going to do." Lainey rubbed the top of her diamond on her wedding ring, like it was a genie that could provide an answer.

"He's not going to leave you high and dry is he?"

"No. Well at least he says he's not, but that stuff can change as soon as the attorneys get involved."

I wanted to offer some reassurance that it wouldn't be that way, but I didn't know Michael. I had only met him a handful of times. "Do you really think it will be like that?"

Lainey looked at me and asked, "Have you ever heard anybody say, 'well the divorce went better than I thought'?"

She was right, and we both knew it. We finished off another bottle of wine, not enough to lighten the load, but enough to get us to sleep.

The next morning Kay made a pitcher of spicy bloody marys. It was too cold to lay out, so we walked on the beach then got in the hot tub. We sat in silence for at least ten minutes before Kay said "God, I didn't realize how much I needed this."

"Me too!" Lainey and I said in unison.

"Jinx, you owe me a coke!" Lainey yelled. We stayed in the hot tub until we all looked like prunes.

Every night we were on the deck by sunset, with more wine. I went for long walks on the beach every day, even though part of me just wanted to sit around feeling sorry for myself. When I was alone with my thoughts I tried to think about what I wanted to do with my life. I was finally ready to take a chance and find my own slice of happiness, create my own destiny by finding fulfillment, yet I had no idea what I wanted. Who gets to the age of thirty without knowing what they want to do with their life?

More than a little grateful that no one seemed to think I should give my blue cheese dressing venture another shot, instead of feeling like a quitter I tried to figure out what to do next. Since we were both unemployed, I thought about asking Lainey if she wanted to go into business with me, but after my last attempt had gone so poorly and without an idea what kind of business to start; I was too embarrassed. Besides, she had enough on her plate. It was obvious that while we were there she was mourning the end of her marriage.

Kay slept late, but my body didn't get the memo that I had been laid off and woke up every morning at six-thirty. And every morning I got up and found Lainey sitting on the deck with a cup of coffee, staring at the ocean. I wanted to say something that would bring her just a little bit of comfort, but even though I had gotten my heart broken with a promise to marry, I hadn't been married. I couldn't imagine what she was going through. I was familiar with the look though, not having energy yet unable to sleep, staring at something far away, but unable to focus your eyes on anything up close. I'd worn it for weeks on end after James cheated on me. Despite my certain ineptitude, after a few mornings I joined her on the deck for coffee in hope that company might suffice even if I didn't have the right words.

I opened the sliding glass door to the deck with the coffee pot in hand. "Want a refill?"

"Don't mind if I do." I filled her cup and mine before sitting down.

"Listen, I can't pretend that I know what you're going through." Lainey went back to staring at the ocean. "I know it's not the same, and what you're going through is probably so much harder than I can even fathom. When James and I broke up, I thought I would never be myself again; like it would take a million years for this ache to fade, this sadness that had invaded my whole body. I just want to say that I know you're going to get through this."

Lainey turned her head, looking me straight in the eye. Even though she looked exhausted, her voice was strong. "Honey, pain is pain. You can't compare grief."

"I just wouldn't want you to think I was trivializing it. James and I didn't even make it to the altar."

"You don't have to make it to the altar to know what it feels like to have your heart broken. The circumstances aren't what give it magnitude. When your world feels like it's been shattered to a million pieces, it doesn't hurt any less or more because of the details." She turned her head back to the sea, and we sat in silence until Kay woke up and joined us.

It's amazing to me that the three of us can always find something to talk about. You would think that at some point we'd run out of things to say, but I guess when you really know each other, there's always more to talk about. The week went by so fast. Before I knew it, it was our last night, sitting on the deck with the last remaining bottle of wine. I felt like a kid who just found out that summer is over, and it's back to school on Monday.

Kay said, "You know, when I think of being old, I think of the three of us, still on a porch somewhere, probably a nursing home."

"What about Jill?" I asked.

"She'll be there too." Lainey answered with a smile. "I just wonder where we'll be a year from now."

Kay said, "Hopefully at the beach. Everything is nicer with the sound of waves as background music. You two will have your mojos back, and be better than ever."

"What about you, Kay? What do you want this year?" I asked.

"I guess I just want everybody to be happy. And…I want to be in love. I'm ready. I'm tired of being single, tired of dating. I can't remember the last time I met somebody that I was excited about. It seems like now that I'm thirty-five, every guy I meet is married or divorced with kids. I don't think I want kids, much less somebody else's kids, but I haven't even liked anybody enough for it to be an issue."

"I want kids," Lainey said "and now I'm thirty-six, with a divorce looming. I don't even want to think about it, but I have to because by the time I'm even ready to start dating again...God, I can't even imagine being back out there. I thought I was finally done with dating. I'm going to be old, as in 'get your eggs frozen' old."

"That's not true." I said.

"How do you figure?" Lainey asked. I thought Kay would chime in, but she was waiting for an answer too.

"I don't know, but these days a lot of people are waiting until later in life to have kids."

"Yeah, and they're having six babies at a time because of fertility treatments!" Lainey yelled, her eyes wide enough that she could have given birth through them.

"At least you're normal," I said. "When I tell people I don't want to have kids, they look at me like I don't like puppies or something. I just can't get excited about having something that shits its pants."

Lainey raised her eyebrows. "You used to shit your pants, Missy."

"And I stopped, thank God."

Kay looked at me, "Really? Remember when you went on that raw food diet?"

"That doesn't count. It was an isolated incident."

We had finished off the wine, so Kay and Lainey went inside to see what our options were from the liquor cabinet. Lainey's in-laws had told her that we could help ourselves, but we waited until it was our last resort. They returned shortly with glasses and a pitcher of something remarkably similar to hunch punch. Kay said, "It's not the best but it's drinkable."

I was flipping through O Magazine, and it had pictures of one of her houses in it. "I wish I could go live with Oprah."

Kay shook her head and made a face I'm all too familiar with which annoys the crap out of me. Our mother could have trademarked it, the knowing look as she shakes her head back and forth. Our mother may have moved two hours away, but she's alive and well and I don't need Kay acting like she's got it all figured out when she's only three years older than me. "Cate, I do not understand your fascination with that woman."

"I get it." Lainey tried to back me up.

"I'm not fascinated with her. Well, maybe a little bit, but mainly I just like her. She really is a good person. And how often do the good people get to be at the top? Perfect example…all those socialites with reality TV shows, pieces of shit, getting paid to do nothing. If you've watched even five minutes of those shows, you know they're not good people. Then there's Oprah who works her ass off and on top of that, tries to make a difference in the world. So every time I see her I get to see the good girl win for a change, and she wins so big!"

"You know she's not perfect." Kay was still making the face.

"The fact that she's human, that she's got flaws like the rest of us, that's exactly what makes her perfect."

Lainey piped in like she always does when Kay and I get snippy with each other. "You don't have to convince me. I feel ya. I would love to move in with Oprah."

"She's got a bunch of houses, and they're probably so big she wouldn't even know I was there. If she would let me move in, adopt me for a while, I could have fancy gourmet meals, Bob Greene approved. I'd probably lose weight. I could play with her dogs since my place is too small to get my own dog. I could help with her gardens. I bet every bed has incredible sheets. My life could be filled with her favorite things, like she had on her show every year. Everything would be different. I definitely wouldn't sit around and cry about how I wasted three-hundred and fifty dollars on a Kitchen Aid mixer that I no longer have a use for, or sit around bundled up in three layers of clothes because I'm worried about the gas bill. I could figure out what to do with my life."

Kay said, "I hate to point out the obvious…" I was afraid she was going to rain on the parade in my head and say that Oprah isn't trying to adopt me, but she didn't. "If Oprah adopted you, or let you move in with her or whatever, she would probably give you a job too."

We stayed up too late, drinking too much, and I realized I wasn't the only one who didn't want our escape to end. The next morning when we packed the car to leave, I was expecting the return trip to be typical, feeling like it takes so much longer to get home than it does to get somewhere good. To my surprise it went by faster. I thought Kay was just being bossy when she said that I should take what I wanted to find at Oprah's house and find a way to incorporate it in my own life, but she had some really good points. She said if I wanted to play with dogs, I could volunteer at an animal shelter. While she drove and Lainey slept, I made a list of all the things I would like about living with Oprah. Obviously leaving out the best stuff like actually living with Oprah, the chef prepared meals, and the sweet-dream inducing fancy sheets, but keeping what I could manage on my own. I didn't have a plan exactly, but I had a few ideas, which was more than I had on the ride down.

CHAPTER 6

Dear Oprah,

I think of what your life must be like and picture you surrounded by things that are lush and beautiful. In this month's edition of O Magazine, there were pictures you had taken of your perfect lazy Sunday. There were gorgeous pictures from your house, things you love, including one of your dogs sleeping in the shade. I am ashamed to admit that I envy your dogs. I'm sure that their life is so much better than mine. I'm trying not to complain and be proactive. After seeing the show you had on The Secret, I've gone through another magazine (I would never cut out the pages of O) and clipped pictures of things that I want in my life so I can visualize what I want and bring it to me. Not every picture is a thing exactly. I took one from an ad for a beach resort, and although I would like to go there, it represents tranquility to me. My budget is too tight for me to get a nice cork board for the pictures like you had on the show, so I'm just putting them on a mirror.

Regards,

Cate

P.S. I hope this doesn't sound weird, but I also put a picture of you on the mirror. It represents my search for an authentic life.

After creating my very own picture collage to represent what I want out of life, I felt so good that I tried to get Kay to make one too. She said she wants to fall in love, and I don't see why the same principles wouldn't work for her. She said that one silly Sanders sister is enough, but maybe she'll change her mind when it works for me.

Since I need to stay busy, just as much as I need to try to create my own Oprah-esque existence, I have found ways to do both. Kay said I should cook for myself as if I'm cooking for Oprah, with fresh healthy gourmet meals. Since I still can't stomach extended time in my disaster kitchen, that will have to wait.

I have been accepted as a volunteer for the Golden Retriever Rescue Center, where I will be donating two hours of my time a day. It will be great to play with the dogs, and I can walk them for exercise. Thanks to the broken beer bottle I stepped on a year ago, I'm current on my tetanus shot and can start tomorrow. Since I don't have a yard, I looked into the community garden options but the two nearby are filled with stinky frizzy haired people wearing Birkenstocks. It's for the best since I found a better option in the online Want Ads. There's a florist looking for a part-time delivery driver. This would put me in proximity to flowers, and in addition to albeit a minuscule income; wherever I go people will be happy to see me. I have an interview today at four. I should conserve funds by staying in, but I'm going to meet Jill afterwards.

When I got to the floral shop there was a small woman with dark hair pulled back standing behind the counter, sticking yellow roses into a cube of green Styrofoam. "Hi" I said, "my name is Cate Sanders." She looked at me with no trace of recognition on her face. "I'm here for the interview."

She grabbed some irises and said, "Oh, I'm so sorry I totally forgot you were coming. Nice to meet you. I'm Betty. I'm afraid we're going to have to talk while I work on this arrangement. Ever since word got out that Reverend Walker passed, I've been slammed with orders."

"Oh." I hadn't thought about funeral flowers, and I didn't want to say that I'd never heard of Reverend Walker since she said it like I should have.

"Tell me about your experience. Have you worked for a florist before?"

"No, but I love flowers." She looked up at me, and I could tell that wasn't the response she was looking for. "Um, I've been in marketing for the past twelve years, but I got laid off. I thought this would be a nice change."

"So, you're looking for something temporary?" Her eyebrows were pinched together so I knew that I still wasn't making any progress.

"No, I mean, kind of. I don't know what I want to do." Realizing that I had started to slouch, I stood up straight and made an effort to keep my shoulders back.

"Maybe I want to be a florist, and this would be a good place to start."

I thought she was going to tell me to go ahead and let the door hit me on my way out, when she said, "How big is your truck?"

I figured I didn't hear her correctly, so I asked "Truck?"

"Your truck, how big is it?" As I stared at her blankly, she said, "You want to deliver flowers and you don't even have a truck, a van?"

"No. I guess I thought I would deliver them in my car." She was looking at me like I was so stupid that it started to piss me off, "or that for eight dollars an hour, you would provide a vehicle."

"Well you thought wrong." She went back to her floral arrangement.

I stood there for a minute, until it became clear that she wasn't going to say anything else. My throat was so dry, I had to clear it just to say "Well thank you for your time." without making a croaking noise. She didn't even look up.

I got to my car, thoroughly pissed and ready to meet Jill for a drink or five. Before I could even light a cigarette, Betty was at my window. I rolled it down reluctantly, certain that if she commented on my BMW convertible being a ridiculous delivery car, I would go off on her. I was already yelling at her in my head, *That's right lady! I wasn't just in marketing; I was a successful marketing executive! I'm not beneath delivering your stupid ass flowers, I should be above it!*

"Listen, I'm really sorry," she started. "I've been here since five this morning, and I didn't mean to take it out on you."

I started to say it was okay, but I read that people treat you based on how you allow yourself to be treated. Now I'm trying to pay close attention to make sure that I'm sending out the right signals. So I said, "Apology accepted." instead.

"My mom is a gardener, I use some of her flowers here, and she needs some part-time help too. I think it's only 2 days a week, but if you want I can give her your information." Hoping that her earlier behavior wasn't indicative of her mother's disposition, I said I would like that. Who knows, with an actual gardener this could be even better. My collage was working out already, so there was even more of a reason to have drinks with Jill.

Betty's mother must have really needed help because she called while we were out. I didn't pick up since I didn't recognize the number. Her voicemail was short and said to come by anytime tomorrow before two o'clock, and she gave an address.

I told Jill about my progress, that I was starting tomorrow as a volunteer at the animal rescue center, and possibly going to have a part-time job. "Well, it's good for you to get out of the house, and I have good news too! Drinks are on me, I'm getting a promotion!"

"That's great. I didn't know you were up for one."

"I didn't think it would go through, so I wasn't going to mention it."

"Why not? Just because I got laid off, you don't have to hide your successes. I'm happy for you."

Jill was so gracious about her promotion, I tried to enjoy it for her. Mostly I felt like a mooch of a best friend, like I should be capable of buying the celebratory drinks.

The next morning I hurried to the Golden Retriever Animal Rescue to start my first day as a volunteer. I was dressed in my Nike tennis shoes and a warm-up suit, ready to walk dogs. When I got there, I was surprised that I didn't see any dogs. A peppy woman named Alexis greeted me and showed me to a back office. "Make yourself at home." She said. "I started the rescue a few years ago. My husband Bill and I started it together, but now that he travels a lot for work, I'm running it by myself. It has grown into a full operation, so I need to get things more organized." She was enviably thin in Seven jeans and a pressed button-down shirt, with shoulder length blonde hair that was undoubtedly the product of a pricey salon. I couldn't help but notice the enormous diamond on her wedding ring. It had to be three carats.

"Where are the dogs?" I asked.

"They're in the kennel. This is the office, which is where you'll be. As soon as we get your waiver signed, we'll get you started." She handed me a pen and piece of paper.

"You rescue them, and put them in a kennel?"

Alexis laughed, "Oh no, it's our kennel. That's where we put the dogs that haven't found foster homes yet, which is where you come in!" She motioned to an enormous stack of papers. "There's the paperwork for our foster families. We're trying to create a computer database, so it will be easier to keep track of them and make matches. Can I get you a cup of coffee or something? Or are you ready to dive in?" The door opened behind her, and a guy walked in, ruggedly handsome with a strong jaw and wearing a fitted shirt over an athletic build. He could have been straight out of the Eddie Bauer catalogue. "This is Todd." Alexis said. He lifted his chin in my direction, as he set something on the table and walked back out. "He helps out at the kennel."

I shifted my weight on my heavily cushioned tennis shoes, and tried to conceal my disappointment. "Um, when do I get to see the dogs, you know play with them or walk them?"

Alexis turned the smile down a notch, but I still noticed how white her teeth were. "You said on your application that you wanted to help out in any way. This is what we need, paperwork onto the computer."

"Right," I said, thinking that I should have said that I needed exercise and time with dogs. Reminding myself that as a volunteer this isn't about my needs, I regrouped. "I just want you to know that I would love to see the dogs too, you know, whenever you need that too."

Alexis seemed to buy it. "Ok, well, coffee and water are in the next room, so help yourself, and just give me a shout if you have any questions." She smiled and disappeared around the corner. I looked at the massive stack of papers, and decided that I indeed needed coffee. There were cute mugs to the side of the coffee maker, all with pictures of golden retrievers. I grabbed one with a photo of a sleeping puppy that was adorable enough to have starred in a toilet paper commercial.

Must be nice, puppy life, I thought as I poured the coffee. I made my way back to the office and sat down, as ready as I was going to be to get to work. As I picked up the first form from the stack, I must have knocked the ones below. The papers started flying out from under it. I put my hands out to grab them, and felt the stinging pain on my fingers as I was the instant recipient of at least ten simultaneous paper cuts. "Shit!" I yelled, dropping every piece of sharp paper as if it was a shard of glass.

"Everything ok in here?" Alexis returned as quickly as she had left.

"Yep" I grimaced, "just paper cuts."

I thought she was going to help me or at least ask if I needed a band aid when she said in a sing-song voice, "Cate, we try to watch our language here."

"Sorry", I said wondering who the hell "we" included.

"You never know when there could be kids here, and even when there aren't, no one likes a potty mouth."

"Right," I wondered if I'd stepped into a foreign world, a land where people use the term 'potty mouth' with a straight face. "Um, ok then, I guess I'll just get back to it." Alexis eyed the papers on the floor before she left the room. I started picking them up, the devil papers, wishing that I had gloves on. I made two piles, so they wouldn't be towering again, positioned for an errant elbow to send them toppling over. I looked at the clock. Ten minutes I had been there. Ten long minutes, and they had two hours of my time, five days a week, as I had stated on the form. I wanted a cigarette, although I didn't have to ask Alexis to know that in her world ashtray mouth is probably akin to potty mouth. I started to drink my coffee, which was so hot that I spewed it all over the computer and keyboard. *SHIT!* I yelled in my head with clenched fists and teeth. I could already feel a scalded thin layer of skin starting to pucker on the roof of my mouth. Afraid that Alexis would magically appear at the thoughts from a potty mouth brain, I grabbed Kleenex from my purse and frantically wiped coffee off the computer screen.

When the coast was clear, I tiptoed into the room with the coffee pot and grabbed napkins to get the remaining coffee splatter off the keyboard. I dabbed at the papers which now looked like they'd been sprayed by a mud puddle. An hour later I had finally made progress. I sorted the foster homes into stacks; vacancy, no vacancy. Vacancies were divided by what I figured must be pertinent information 'children in the home', 'other pets' (which was two stacks, those with cats, those with dogs), and 'seniors' since older dogs might be better with older people. I was close to creating files in the computer, when I realized I didn't know what kind of database they were going to use, but my two hours were up. I looked for Alexis. Her Range Rover was still outside, but she was nowhere to be found in the small renovated house they were using as an office. I waited ten minutes, and when there was still no sign of her, I left a note. It read, "Done for the day. I'll be back at the same time tomorrow. Need to know what kind of database you're using, so I can enter them accordingly. Thanks!" I thought about putting a smiley face on the note, figuring Alexis did that sort of thing, but it didn't feel like me. After the whole potty mouth thing, I figured she knew that.

I decided to head straight to my next gig partially because I wanted to get it over with, and partially because I was afraid if I went home first, it would be even harder to get motivated to drag myself over there.

When I got to the address Betty's mom had left on my voicemail, I wasn't sure I was at the right place. It was a bungalow style house, old Atlanta. Charming and quaint, it was the kind of house I had thought James and I would be living in. I felt a surge of annoyance, as I thought about how different my life was supposed to be now. Reminding myself that he wasn't the one for me, since the right one would never fuck his boss, I took a deep breath and walked to the door. I knocked twice, waiting between each one, but no answer. Thinking that she had forgotten I was coming and wasn't home, I was relieved that I could leave. I knocked one more time for good measure. As I turned to walk back to my car, the door opened to a woman with a round face peering out from a floppy straw hat. "You, my dear, must be Cate." She had a warm welcoming smile and bright blue eyes, younger than I would have imagined since Betty had to be over fifty. "Come on back," she motioned with her free hand, the other was holding a small shovel, "I'll show you the garden." The house was open, with a living room, flowing into a dining room, followed by the kitchen. There were plants everywhere, tropical looking trees in every corner and hanging baskets in nooks around the kitchen. Through the kitchen, big glass doors opened into an enormous back yard, much bigger than what normally accompanies houses of that size. "If you're thirsty, I've got a pitcher of sun tea that should be brewed by now."

"I'm fine, thank you." I said, figuring that even though Betty must have told her I didn't have experience, no reason to get comfortable until we established that I had the job.

She stepped through the doors and before I could follow her, she was back with a pitcher of sun tea. "Have some anyway. It's good for you." She had small green leaves in her hand. She dropped them in the pitcher, before pouring it over two glasses filled with ice. "Mint,j" she answered my silent question, "it's so refreshing." She handed me a glass and took a sip of the other one. "I'm Vivian," she said, "but you probably sorted that out already."

"Nice to meet you, Vivian." I said.

"Come on outside." she said as she opened a drawer and grabbed a pack of cigarettes. "You smoke?" I asked.

"Don't give me a lecture. I'm too old for lectures, and I don't give a shit."

"Me either!" I replied. "I mean I'm not too old for lectures, but I smoke."

"Oh good," she said, "It's horrible you know." Vivian handed me a cigarette and walked outside. I eagerly followed. There were plants everywhere. Pots inside the perimeter of the deck, baskets on the railing. There was foliage and flowers everywhere I looked, making it hard to focus on any one thing.

There was a glass patio table on the back deck, she sat down and lit her cigarette before handing me the lighter. It wasn't the cheap colorful plastic kind like I get at the gas station. It was silver with her initials engraved on it. "So Cate, tell me about yourself."

I lit mine, and took a drag before answering. Her cigarettes were long and thin, as dainty as a cigarette could be. "I got laid off, and now I'm trying to figure out what to do with my life. So I'm looking for something part-time to keep busy, and I like flowers." Since Betty had probably told her as much, I didn't try to sell myself. When Vivian didn't say anything, I wondered if I was mistaken. "I'm a quick learner, and I work hard." I added in hope that this wouldn't be a rerun of my meeting with Betty.

Vivian looked at me for a moment before saying, "What about you, though? What do you want to do with your life?"

"I don't know." I answered before I jumped at the feel of something warm and wet on my wrist. "Oh shit!" I yelled as I looked down to see a big black dog, a face like a baby bear with short round ears and a fuzzy tail like a squirrel's.

Vivian laughed. "That's Buddy. He's a lover, just can't help it, giving people kisses before he even introduces himself."

I tried to compose myself, petting his head, sending his tail into a wagging frenzy. "Aw, he's so sweet. His ears feel like velvet, they're so soft. I could love on him all day." I said, as Buddy licked my wrist again.

"Well, I'm glad you like him. That's the only requirement for the job if you want it." I didn't know a single detail, but was so pleasantly surprised by Vivian that it didn't matter to me what the job was. I quickly answered, "I want it."

"Pays eight dollars an hour, same as Betty's, but I only need you here about ten hours a week. Whether you want to do it all in one day, or spread it out, it's fine with me either way."

"What kind of help do you need?"

"I just need somebody to pitch in. It's gotten to be too much, but I'm not ready to retire. In a few years I'll probably limit my gardening to my personal enjoyment, but for now I still like having it as a business too." Vivian took a short puff off of her cigarette, even looking graceful while smoking. I watched her, hoping that some of her mannerisms would rub off on me. Maybe I could be the girl who wears a white shirt that doesn't have coffee stains or whatever was breakfast on the front of it. "It's a good way to find yourself," she said, "playing in the dirt." I wondered if it was obvious that I was lost. Vivian seemed to read my mind. "It's alright, love. Everyone loses their way now and again."

After we smoked, Vivian took me through the garden, explaining that she had bought two lots, planning on expanding the house someday. As each year came and went, she outgrew her garden space. So she decided to turn the second lot into a garden. There was a greenhouse at the edge of the other lot. The glass looked like it was frosted with moisture. The garden space was so beautiful, the way she had rows of flowers mixed with the vegetables.

"Before you go," she said, "let's get you something to grow at home." Vivian walked into the kitchen and came back with one of her hanging baskets from inside. "This is a Wandering Jew."

It was a big plant with purple leaves that looked like they had been painted around the edges with pale green.

"I can't take that." I said, taken aback by her generosity.

Vivian handed me a small terracotta pot with potting mix in it. "It's staying here, but we're going to make you your own." She handed me pruning shears, and was holding another pair in her hands. "This is like you. We can take parts of it and given a little attention, it will grow into its own. " She began to snip the longer vines, showing me where to cut. When we had about fifteen vines, she showed me how to gently place them in the dirt. "Now when you get this home just spritz it with water, but not so much that it drains. It has everything it needs to develop roots. And not only do plants help the air quality of your home, it's good to have something to take care of."

I loved the easiness of her voice, and learning about the plants. If Vivian didn't have to leave for a doctor's appointment, I could have stayed all day.

The next morning I headed straight to the animal rescue. I wore my sneakers and a warm up-suit again, in the off chance that I'd get to go to the kennel and walk the dogs. Alexis wasn't there, but the front door was open. She had left me a note on the computer screen. It was longer than the one I'd left her, and certainly devoid of smiley faces. "Cate, there isn't a database yet. I need you to create one. I have an important appointment this morning, and won't be here to walk you through it. Your application said you have database management experience, so you should be able to figure it out. Also, if you could try to keep your work space clean, that would be great. I need to devote my time to finding forever homes for the dogs and can't spend my time cleaning up after you."

After making sure that I was indeed there by myself, I yelled to no one "WHAT THE HELL?!" I couldn't believe that while I was volunteering my time, she was belittling my efforts. My experience is in analyzing pre-existing marketing databases, not creating doggy databases! It was all I could do to keep myself from walking right out the door. With one glance at the daily calendar and the irresistibly sweet face of the golden retriever in the picture, I decided to stay. I wasn't going to let some Junior League type bitch run me off.

I didn't have a clue how to create a database, so I organized each application with key words. I had almost finished entering the information from one stack when I heard the beep from Alexis's car alarm. I tried to look engrossed in the computer screen so I wouldn't have to talk to her. It was pointless since she came in chatting away on her cell phone. As much as I tried to tune her out, her sing song voice permeated the room, "Bill's firm is already donating a number of items for the silent auction...This fundraiser needs some high profile names. I can't carry the whole thing by myself again...What about Mimi Jackson as a co-host? I chaired her leukemia fundraiser last year, it's the least she can do..." I thought I had managed to be invisible, but she came in and propped her small ass on the edge of the desk, with a tight smile in my direction. As she blabbered on, I couldn't help but notice her nails, perfect French manicure. There was a familiar fragrance too. As it dawned on me that it was the smell of grapefruit sugar scrub, I realized what her important appointment was. That bitch had been at the day spa!

I was so pissed I didn't notice she'd gotten off the phone until she said, "Cate, I need you to call Le Chanterelle and reserve space for the fundraiser. It's a nice French restaurant down by..."

I cut her off, "I know Le Chanterelle." She looked taken aback; either surprised that I knew a nice restaurant or she'd never been interrupted before.

"Good." She pursed her lips and got her ass off the desk. "We need space for a hundred, and get them to send over sample menus, so I can make the selections."

She left the room before I could respond, which was undeniably for the best. I sat there wondering how I had become a poorly treated administrative assistant, who worked for free. When she popped her head back in to check my progress, I asked if the event was black tie. I was going to manage to work my Gucci dress into the conversation, pretending I needed to pick it up from the cleaners as if it had ever been worn.

"Yes," she answered "but don't worry, I don't expect you to attend." She eyed me up and down, the way Barbara used to do, but with a fake grin. "You're fine here, in your sporty attire."

Her cell phone rang, and she left the room. I tried to stay calm, taking deep breaths. I shouldn't go to Le Chanterelle for at least a year anyway since the chef had been at my blue cheese fiasco. Deep breaths didn't work, and my two hours were almost up. I left, without leaving the note that I had written in my head. It wouldn't have fit on a post-it anyway, a tracing of my hand, all knuckles except for my middle finger.

CHAPTER 7

Dear Oprah,

Yesterday I was watching a rerun of when you had Reggie Wells, your make-up artist, on the show. I loved him! I could use a Reggie in my life, and not just because I need someone to transform my face and turn the bags under my eyes into smooth skin before applying perfect eyelashes. Like every other single girl in the world, without the companionship of a gay man, I might as well be a woman without an island. He was talking about not complaining and focusing on being happy, which is something I'm working on too. Please give him an extra hug today, from me.

Regards,

Cate

P.S. If you ever do an O makeover in Atlanta, I'd like to be first on the list for an appointment with Reggie.

After I left the animal rescue and bitchy Alexis, I was all wound up with nowhere to go. As much as I wanted it to be five o'clock or close enough to justify happy hour, it wasn't quite noon. These are the moments when you know you should exercise, unwinding with yoga or releasing tension with a kickboxing class. Unfortunately these are also the moments when those options are the least appealing, like when I was a kid and craving something sweet and my mom would tell me to eat an apple. I wished I could just show up at Vivian's; absorb some of her peaceful nature into the petulance that had taken over me, but I wasn't due back until tomorrow.

In the spirit of trying to create my own peace, my own Oprah-esque existence, I decided to go to Home Depot and get more plants for my place. I walked into the garden area, overwhelmed by the selection which was foreign to me. As I looked through the plants, I pulled out the plastic labels inserted in the dirt and read. Full sun, partial light, foliage, humidity, pruning requirements, there were so many things to learn. I looked around for a brochure, some sort of dictionary guide to decipher the labels.

Not seeing anything, I put an Aloe Vera plant in my cart. At least I knew what it was. As a child, I had seen pictures of the plant on bottles of Aloe Vera juice which crowded our refrigerator. My mom had been a Lady Love representative, and their mainstay was peddling the concoction. African violets were on sale, feature plant of the week. I didn't know anything about them, but liked the name and the little purple flowers.

"Need some help?" I looked up to see a smiling, tall, gorgeous man behind the deep voice. Despite the fact that he clearly worked there, wearing an orange apron and work gloves, the ridiculous reflex of a scowl had already crept on my face. Not seeming to notice, he said, "Good choice, African violets are my boyfriend's favorite." My face relaxed from the knee jerk reaction to a sheepish smile. It's not a reaction from a misguided belief that every man is hitting on me. I know better. It's a protection mechanism to keep me clear of men like James. After the break up, I started reading a self help book and now understand why I have since kept a hostile distance from men. If the book hadn't been so fucking boring, I would've finished it and learned how to better develop my coping skills.

The guy was standing there, smiling at me with his eyebrows raised, and I realized that I hadn't said a word. "Oh, um, yeah" I stammered, "I could use some help. I need one more plant, something tall, but not like a tree because it's going to be indoors."

"Oh-kaaay", he said as he turned his head, looking at the options around us.

"I guess it's obvious that I don't know anything about plants."

"Do I know you?" he asked, looking back at me. "I feel like I know you from somewhere."

I shook my head. Gay or straight, there was no way I would have forgotten that guy. He was beyond handsome, like a model, the kind of person who doesn't walk among us in real life. He would have fit in wearing boxer briefs on a billboard in Times Square.

"You're Cate Sanders! Oh my God, from high school! I used to sit behind you in home room!"

I stood there baffled, wondering if the little pot I smoked in college had obliterated my memory.

"I'm Christian, Christian Selig." I remembered Christian Selig. My shock quickly turned into a sense of despair at the injustice. He had gone from gangly and pimple faced to tall, tanned, toned, and flawless-skin gorgeous. Here I was the same, except for the beginning of fine lines on my face, boobs that would no longer pass the pencil test and an extra thirty pounds.

"Wow!" I said, "You look incredible. Sorry for the memory lapse, it has been a long time."

Despite the fact that we had hardly known each other, he hugged me like an old friend. "So, what are you doing here?" Christian asked.

I gestured at my cart and said, "Getting plants, and I need something that I can't kill…" but the truth came out like I was regurgitating. "To be completely honest, I wouldn't be here at all, but I couldn't think of anything else to do." I shook my head at my failed attempt at honesty. "That's not true either. I wanted to have drinks, but it's too early in the day since I'm not an alcoholic, and there isn't anyone who could meet me for drinks this early anyway. I got laid off a while back and all of my friends are nine to fivers." I sighed. Although I was sure I sounded like a complete nut job, it felt good to let it all hang out.

He didn't respond the way I would have expected, scooting away and saying it had been nice to see me. He smiled big, and said teasingly, "Well, first things first. Let's get you a plant you can't kill. I've got the perfect thing. It's tall, but don't worry, not a tree." He walked over to the next aisle and pointed at something that was just perfect, dark green tall straight pointy leaves with yellow vertical lines on them.

"It is perfect! What is it?"

"Snake grass, but also known as mother-in-law's tongue because you can't stop it, it just grows." He put it in my cart, and then walked me over to an area with pots. With the clichéd but much appreciated gay man's style, he helped me pick out pots that were the perfect contrasting colors and designs for my Aloe Vera and African Violets. When he took off his apron, telling me that his shift was over, I tried to hide my disappointment. I knew it was pathetic. I didn't think we were going to hang out at Home Depot all day.

"It was really good to see you." I said.

"You too, Cate." Christian started to walk away, but then turned and asked, "Hey, do you like sushi?"

"I love sushi!" I said, feeling a twinge of guilt, remembering that I still hadn't called Rachel back. Before I got laid off, we went out for sushi every Friday for lunch.

"You know, it may be early for happy hour, but not for sushi and sake. I'm free. If you want we could go to Niko's..."

I interrupted, "I'd love to!"

I was so excited. I love gay men, and I swear every woman needs at least one in their life. I'm not a fag hag, but I'd make a great one. Ever since my dear friend Robert moved to Miami two years ago there's been a hole in my world. While he could never be replaced,

I've needed this, the attention of a man who has no interest in sleeping with me.

Niko's wasn't exactly in my budget, but how could I refuse Christian's invitation? We sat at the corner of the sushi bar. My mouth watered as I eyed the perfect pieces of white tuna, salmon, and yellowtail on a big purple radish, cut into the shape of a flower. I was thrilled to hear that Christian likes his sake hot. I don't care that high quality sake should be served chilled, I like cheap warm sake. We started eating seaweed salad when out of nowhere Christian said, "Did you know I had a crush on you in high school? I wanted to ask you to prom, but I never got up the nerve."

"What?" I pointed to the slippery strands of seaweed that had just gone from my chopsticks to the table. "Look what you did. You made me drop good seaweed. What are you talking about? You're gay, and don't tell me your bi because I don't believe in that. People cannot go around monopolizing both genders."

Christian laughed. "I'm not bi. Back then I knew I was gay, but hadn't really accepted myself yet and had this whole theory on how my sexuality was on a continuum. I was attracted to you."

"Really? So you were already attracted to men, but you were attracted to me? I must have missed the effect I was going for with the hot rollers."

"Yeah, really. Let me think of how to explain it," he said before dipping a spicy tuna roll in soy sauce. "At that age it was different. I hadn't fully given in to who I was going to be. I mean, I felt it, but I also had some interest in girls. Every morning I sat behind you, and you did something for me. Your hair smelled like cherries or something. I was definitely attracted to you. Maybe I thought about it more because at the time I thought you might be my chance…to be...normal."

"Oh Christian!" I leaned in and hugged him, trying not to tear up. "I think that is the nicest thing anyone has ever said to me."

"So you can imagine my surprise today when there you were, in Homo Depot."

"Homo Depot?"

"That's what we call that location. It's midtown, where all the hot gay guys get their materials."

"That's why you work there?"

"No, but it doesn't hurt. This is just temporary. I decided to go back to school full time. I'm getting my master's degree in Landscape Architecture."

Hoping he would expound upon that, so I wouldn't have to talk about my life, I put a piece of the spicy tuna roll in my mouth. It didn't work. Before I could even start chewing he said, "So I would have thought you'd be married with kids by now."

Still chewing, I shook my head.

"Divorced?"

I shook my head again as I sipped my sake.

"It's a long story." I said. "I'm just glad to be exactly where I am. Here, with you. And I'm glad that you're not the heart crushing monster from the land of I Can't Keep It In My Pants" I surprised myself with a laugh. "Wait, I guess it's not a long story after all."

"God, Cate, I'm sorry."

I shrugged. "It's been many months, but we were engaged, and he was the third in a string of bad boyfriends. They didn't all cheat, but they were all…" My voice trailed off as I tried to think of how to explain it. "Do you ever watch the TV show Criminal Minds?"

"I love that show!"

"Well, they were all like Shemar Moore."

Christian gave me a side glance and refilled our sake cups. "Um, I'm starting to lose all sympathy for you."

"No, they weren't all look-a-likes. Please, in real life most of the guys who look like that are on your team, way too pretty to be straight. I mean they all had that bad boy quality, that thing where they're all about the chase."

As the sound of the birthday song, with a heavy Japanese accent permeated the restaurant, I began to sing and clap along with the wait staff. Looking around, I didn't see a birthday party. They headed to our end of the bar. "Happy Birthday!" Christian yelled. The waiter placed a big fruity drink in a cup shaped like Bhudda in front of us. I leaned in to Christian. "It's not my birthday." I whispered. He put his arm around me, and pointed to our waiter, in front of us with a Polaroid camera.

"Smile!" Everyone cheered. After the birthday serenade, Christian said he couldn't resist. He had always wanted to try their birthday beverage.

"Sorry," he said. "back to your dating history. The bad boys are fun, but you should only date them, not marry them. So you have a type. That's ok."

"The last three were completely different, not even from the same continents. My fiancée was British, and before him, one was a southern guy, the other was Venezuelan. The only thing they had in common was me. I'm drawn to men who aren't good for me."

Christian held up the Polaroid that had just come into focus. "Look, it's a great picture of you! We look like the perfect couple." He put it in my purse. "Don't worry, Cate. You'll grow out of dating men who aren't good for you."

We finished our sushi and talked. Neither one of us had kept up with people from high school, but we traded stories about the ones we'd run into over the years. Before we left we exchanged numbers and agreed that we had to get together again.

I went home invigorated. It had been a while since I had made a new friend, much less a guy friend. When James and I first started dating, he said that my guy friends weren't really friends; they wanted to sleep with me. After a year of telling him how ridiculous that was; I noticed that they had all slowly disappeared as things got serious with James.

The day had turned out so much better than it had started, I wanted to take my renewed positive energy and focus on moving forward. Since I would have to deal with Alexis again tomorrow, I needed to face the situation head on. It would be an opportunity for growth. Other than Barbara, who I was forced to deal with when she was my boss, I've always avoided women like Alexis. Realizing that dealing with difficult people is part of life, I was determined to adjust my temperament and treat her with diplomacy. After all, I was a new person, the kind of person who has plants. While I would be willing to help out in the office, I wasn't going to put up with any more of her shit and most importantly I wanted to see the dogs. Worst case scenario, I would at least get to see Buddy at Vivian's.

The next day when I went in, Alexis was already there drinking coffee in a Starbucks cup. Aha! I knew there was no way she drank the bitter, acidic swill she had in the coffee pot. With the calm, even voice I had practiced the night before, I said, "Alexis, at some point today, I want to go to the kennel. I'd like to see the dogs that I'm volunteering to help." She reluctantly agreed to take me over there. There was so much hesitation that I wondered if there actually were dogs there.

"Well, there's a lot to do in the office, and we don't have time to waste, but if you insist...we should go now." She looked at her watch. She's the kind of woman, who when everyone else gives up watches since you can just look at your cell phone, will still wear her Cartier. The kennel was right by the office, not even a five minute drive. I figured she was just being difficult, acting like it was a production to take time away from the office work.

There was an empty fenced yard attached to a small building that looked like a little farm house, with a detached garage off to the side. When we walked into the building, a few dogs started barking. We walked into the main room, where there were crates lined up around the side of the walls, making a U shape. Each one had a small piece of paper with their names on it, like nametags.

"We arranged them like this so they can see each other when they're in their crates. They've already been out this morning." Her voice had softened, losing the usual snotty tone that accompanies the sing song way she talks. There was loud thumping, the sound of tails wagging in crates. Out of about thirty crates, only half of them were occupied.

"Do you ever get a full house?" I asked, realizing that I didn't know anything about how the rescue operates.

"Just once, after hurricane Katrina, twelve to fifteen is the usual." She walked over to one of the crates, and opened the door. A ginger hued golden retriever came running out like a bull from a pin. I squatted down to the floor as she came running over, licking my face and knocking me backwards. "Easy Daisy" Alexis said. Whining immediately ensued from the other dogs.

"Can the others come out?" I asked.

"That's not a good idea. It's a bit much unless they're going into the yard." We had only been there a few minutes, but Alexis looked at her watch again. "I guess we have a little time." Looking at one of the other crates, she said, "How about you, Cooper? You want to play for a minute?" She opened Cooper's crate and he came over with the same gusto Daisy had. I didn't care what Alexis thought of me sitting on the floor, letting them lick my face.

Cooper was gorgeous, blonde as he could be with eyes that looked like he was wearing black liquid eye liner. "Cooper is from a really good blood line." Alexis said adding, "He'll go fast." I was glad that he'd find a home soon, but it made me want to hug on Daisy's big neck even more. All of the sweet retriever faces were peering out at me. They looked like they were in doggy prison behind the grated doors of their crates.

I immediately decided that it was worth putting up with all of Alexis's snide remarks if ultimately I was helping them. I would stay with it, and practice on Alexis, giving the signals I'd read about that let people know how you want to be treated. It wasn't long before Alexis checked her watch again, and said we needed to get back. As much as I wanted to tell her that ten more minutes wasn't going to make a difference, I figured that if what I was doing meant the dogs had homes sooner; there was no reason to argue. I would have plenty of other days to play with the dogs and give them the love and attention they deserved.

Not long after we got back to the office, Alexis left. With her out of the office, the time went by faster, as I continued to enter the information into what would hardly pass as a database by any standard. It was motivating to picture the faces of the homeless dogs. I wrapped up for the day, staying a little longer than planned, until it was time to go to Vivian's for gardening 101.

When I got there, I found a note on the door. 'Cate, come on in.' When I walked in I was greeted by the lingering smell of sautéed onion and garlic, and the sound of Ella Fitzgerald's voice in the background. I went to the kitchen, where Vivan was stirring something on the stove top. I got in her line of vision, something l learned from having a mother who startles easily.

"Glad you're here." she said, as she hugged me. Hugging as a standard greeting is one of the best things about living in the south. "I was afraid I wouldn't hear the door over the music."

"I love Ella Fitzgerald." I said.

"You do? I wouldn't think somebody of your generation would recognize her."

"My grandmother was a fan. I love this music, along with Chet Baker, Billie Holiday, Tony Bennett, and Dean Martin. It relaxes me."

"Me too." Vivian was beaming. "I'm just making vegetable soup with the last of the winter crop. I love this time of year, just before spring. And since Atlanta has four proper seasons, you can grow just about anything here if you plan it right." Gesturing at the pot, as she removed her apron, she said, "I can leave this for a bit, so we can get to work." Buddy walked into the kitchen, stretching along the way, like he'd just gotten up from a nap. He started sniffing me all over, undoubtedly smelling Daisy and Cooper on my clothes.

"Want to keep me company, while I take him for a walk?" Vivian asked. I started to say that I could take him, but it occurred to me that Vivian might need company more than she needed help with the garden. I didn't mind, and as I thought about how I had wanted to come here yesterday, I realized that I wanted her company as much as I wanted a part-time job and a garden to tend.

"I would." I answered. Fifteen minutes into our walk, Buddy began to lag behind. "How old is Buddy?"

"He's seven. This is just him being lazy though. He still has the energy of a puppy. He used most of it chasing squirrels and birds this morning. He's a damn good garden dog, always stays between the rows, doesn't dig or trample anything."

I thought about telling Vivian about the animal rescue, but didn't want to think or talk about Alexis so I asked, "What breed is he?"

"He's a mutt, picked him up from the Humane Society when he was just a tiny thing. The whole litter was there, but Buddy was off to the side, the runt who wouldn't fight the others for the food bowl. Something about him was just so gentle; I knew he was the one for me. I looked at him, unable to picture him as a puppy, he had to weigh at least eighty pounds.

After we walked, Vivian and I went into the garden and pulled weeds, removing twigs and leaves as we went. Vivian told me how Betty used to help her when she was little, but by the time she was in high school, she didn't want anything to do with the garden. "There are garden people and cut flowered people. Garden people can be both, but cut flowered people don't like to get in the dirt. Betty is a cut flower person."

I knew exactly what she meant. "My sister, Kay, is a cut flower person."

Vivian didn't say anything for a while, and I got into a rhythm of pulling weeds and tossing twigs. A few minutes later her voice caught me off guard. "You have a sister named Kay?"

"Yes." I answered. She had stopped pulling, and was looking at me.

"So, you're Cate and Kay?" Then I knew where she was going with this.

"Yeah, my mom says our names are very different. Kay is short for Mikayla, and I'm Catherine." Either the sun was in her eyes or she found it as unsatisfactory as we did as children. So I added, "I learned a long time ago, that if you press our mother you're subjecting yourself to a long diatribe. She would tell us that whenever it mattered, like when we were in trouble, she used our full names anyway. Then she'd go on and on, saying that our dad was set on giving us family names, we should thank her every day of our lives that she went with her side of the family. Otherwise we would be named Eugenia and Mildred."

Vivian went back to pulling and said, "Kay and Cate, good names." After an hour, Vivian stood up and picked up her garden stool. "That's enough pulling weeds for one day. If I stay here any longer, my back will be stiff as a board later."

"Do you want me to keep pulling?" I asked.

"Do you know what would be the biggest help…if you would water the garden. My arthritis has been acting up lately, and it's hard on my hands. There are two hoses, one for each side, ready to go."

"Sure," I answered. "I would have thought you had a sprinkler system for a garden this size."

She shook her head no. "Call me old-fashioned." Vivian was heading back to the house, but turned around and called out, "I'll turn the water on. If you notice anything with sagging leaves, that's its way of saying it's extra thirsty." Before I could ask any questions, she was inside.

It took over two hours to water the garden. When I came in, Vivian said we should call it a day. She insisted that I take home a big container of her vegetable soup. By the time I got home, I was worn out, but in a good way, the tired you only get from manual labor. Instead of feeling restless and wanting to go out for cocktails, I took a hot bath and enjoyed the quiet of my condo.

The next morning when I arrived at the animal rescue feeling refreshed and ready to work, there was no sign of Alexis. Time went by quickly and before I knew it my two hours were up. As I moved the last of the stack of paperwork to the other side of the desk I saw a pink post-it note from Alexis. 'Cate, I looked through the database you've created. I thought you would be further along, but it's good that you're not since this is hardly up to par. See me tomorrow.' My face flushed instantly with anger.

She should have told me how she wanted it to begin with, or at least before I wasted another morning of my volunteered time while she was probably at a salon getting a root touch up. As I sat there stewing, I noticed a key ring, marked 'kennel' hanging from a hook on the wall. "Fuck you Alexis." I said to an empty room. "Fuck you." as I grabbed the keys and headed to the kennel. I needed a reminder of why I was putting up with her shit, and without Alexis hovering and checking her watch every two minutes, I had my chance to give all of the dogs some love. I walked in and went straight to the crates, quickly opening each one. There was a puppy in the mix, about thirty pounds or so, with feet too big for her body. I noticed her first because she peed on the floor as she came running over. The dogs alternated between nuzzling each other, and greeting me. It became obvious that I couldn't delay cleaning up the pee. They were running around, and it was only a matter of time before one of them stepped in it. As I walked back to the kitchen for paper towels, I heard soft whimpering. I followed the noise, thinking that maybe there was a sick dog that had been isolated from the others. The closer I got to the noise, I could hear grunting too. Dog fight!

With adrenaline pumping I ran, following the sound into the garage. Frantically looking around, ready to break it up or do whatever was needed, I didn't see any dogs. Then I noticed the back of two bare legs, a hairy naked ass, and long legs wrapped around the back of the waist. I stood there frozen. As he turned his head, I saw that it was Todd with his groin still pumping. Alexis's face looked fiercely over his shoulder, with a vein that looked like it was going to pop out of her forehead. "What are you doing here?!" she demanded.

"Me?" I yelled back. "I came to check on the dogs, to play with them! The better question would be what are you doing here, if it weren't so obvious that you're whoring around!"

"Oh my God, you stupid bitch!" she yelled back. "Me? You're pretending to run an animal rescue while you fuck the dog walker! You've got me doing bullshit grunt work, that you're too lazy or stupid to do, and I don't know which is worse!"

Alexis pushed Todd away from her. She started to jump down from the work bench she was sitting on, but stopped as she looked down, as if she had forgotten that she was naked except for her lacy pink bra. Todd was quickly pulling up his boxers. "Yes, you are a stupid bitch!" She was pointing behind me. "Todd, get them! Todd!"

I turned and saw the dogs running around the other side of the garage. I had left the back door wide open. I went to chase after them. Todd was now running through the front yard in his boxer shorts, catching the dogs one and two at a time and rushing them into the fenced area. Racing after Cooper as he ran across the street, I was chanting in my head, *please don't let him get hit by a car, please don't let him get hit by a car*. He kept looking back at me, with what looked like a huge grin on his face. Clearly enjoying the chase, Cooper kept on running even when we got to woods.

He must have gone almost a mile before he stopped. I dove like superman for him, before he could take off again. I landed right beside him, took hold of his collar, and hugged him. The chanting turned into *thank you, thank you, thank you* while he panted in my ear. It was a long walk back. He was too heavy to carry, so we walked awkwardly with me half bent over holding onto his collar.

When we got to the yard I could see Alexis's Range Rover pulling out from behind the garage. I was going to keep walking, but she pulled up beside me and rolled down her window. Still holding onto Cooper I was unable to stand up straight, but still managed to tilt my head enough to make eye contact.

"Listen here, you little bitch," she seethed, "if I never see you again, it will be too soon."

Hating that I wasn't eye level with her, I said, "Alexis, no one likes a potty mouth." I kept walking, and smiled as Cooper and I made our way back to the fenced area, where Todd stood with all of the other dogs.

CHAPTER 8

Dear Oprah,

I wouldn't want to take anything away from the girls at your school, who are certainly more deserving than I am and have a greater need. Despite that, I can't help wishing that you would adopt me. I feel lost. Look at all you accomplished by the age of thirty-two, yet here I am, a mess on the road to nowhere. I want to be a good person, and I want to do good things. Maya Angelou brilliantly said, "If you don't like something, change it. If you can't change it, change your attitude." I'm sure you've heard this, probably straight from her own mouth. I'm doing my best to follow those pearls of wisdom, don't let my whining give you the wrong impression. Writing to you helps, bringing strength and clarity during these momentary lapses of weakness.

Regards,

Cate

P.S. If by some chance you do want to adopt me, I am available.

After I left the kennel, I went home to clean up before heading out to meet Jill for drinks. After chasing Cooper through the woods, I looked like an unholy mess with a hole in the knee of my warm-up pants and a few scrapes to show for my efforts. When I got to the pub Jill wasted no time, pointing out that life's too short to needlessly put up with the likes of Alexis. "I know," I said. "But I'm starting to feel like it's me, like I have bad juju or something."

"Juju? What the hell is Juju?"

"It's like karma, but for other people..." I tried to remember where I'd heard the term, and couldn't recall the source anymore than a way to elaborate on the meaning. "Maybe you know bad juju when you've got it. And I've got it. I should go down to Little Five Points, find some mystical store and a voodoo woman to fix it."

"That's hullaballoo." Before I could ask Jill continued, "I don't know exactly what that means either but while you're throwing out words like juju, it seems appropriate to me."

"Well what am I supposed to think? I can't get anything right these days. I'm an ass clown without a calling."

"You're supposed to keep going. A couple of small bumps in the road don't mean anything. What happened to that long list of ideas you had? Remember? All the things you wanted to do?"

"They all seem stupid now. How did I think I was going to walk into a different life? "

"They're not stupid. You need to get back to where you started and have a little faith in your sign. So what if things aren't exactly what you pictured? You wanted a garden and time with a dog, and now you've got Vivian and Buddy. That has to mean something to you."

Jill gave me a much needed boost of confidence. We stayed out later than we should on a week night, but trivia was starting and Jill wanted to play. I didn't have anywhere to be in the morning, and reasoned that maybe we could win our next bar tab since it was getting hard to justify going out for drinks without real income.

The next morning I woke up with a slight hangover, and my despondency had returned. I had nowhere to be, and all of my friends were at work. Instead of being productive, I laid on the couch watching TV. As I flipped channels, I stopped on a Lifetime movie about Coco Chanel. As I watched, sipping coffee, her story unfolded as she started her design business with hats. It was another sign. Jill's words from the night before kept going through my mind, "Cate, if you want to find the path for you, focus on that. Don't waste energy on what didn't work. Think about what you haven't tried yet."

Coco started making hats from her lover's house. Yes, she had a background as a seamstress, but I didn't want to actually make the hats. I wanted to create jewelry for hats, which could be worn separately or together. I had seen the jewelry that people made from beads. I could do this! You can't make people sick from hats, so worst case scenario; it would have to work out better than my last venture. I started making a list, determined to look at every possible angle and prevent any foreseeable problems.

I looked online for hat wholesalers and settled on a plain black straw hat, perfect with spring approaching. I measured my head, deciding it was average in size, making sure I would get the fit I envisioned. I could get ninety six hats for just under four hundred dollars. I hadn't factored all of the startup costs into my small budget, but how else was I going to get my new business and life off the ground? After all, the movie showed Coco in her shop without heat, wearing a blanket like a shawl around her shoulders and look at her empire now! I continued my internet search, looking up information on making beaded jewelry.

As I typed, I noticed that the fleshy part of my right palm was tender. Remembering what Vivian had said about watering the garden being too much for her hands, I couldn't imagine how sore it would be on top of arthritis. I decided to add 'volunteer free watering service for Vivian' to my growing To Do List.

There was more than I would have thought to beaded jewelry design: classes, patterns for purchases, downloaded instructions for a fee. Needing to conserve my resources, I decided that a book from Barnes & Noble would give me all the information I needed at the lowest cost.

With Christian's eye for style, I decided he would be the perfect shopping partner for my beads. I found a bead shop in town and called him with an invitation for drinks in exchange for help with bead choices and a trip to Barnes & Noble. He instantly agreed to help but couldn't go out for drinks afterwards, insisting that he had to go to the gym. Officially done with my 'sporty attire', I dressed for creative inspiration, putting on a vintage Betsey Johnson corset over a fitted long-sleeve tee, jeans and tall boots. We met at the bookstore, where Christian greeted me, "Hello, hot mama! Corset becomes you!"

"Betsey Johnson," I said, "Or as I like to call her, the woman behind the only brave fashion choices I make!" Christian perused the fiction section while I searched for the perfect how-to guide. Settling on a book for all skill levels, we were ready to head to the bead store. Keeping in mind that the beads would be against black straw hats, we went for a complimentary mix. I was overwhelmed by the variety: pressed, Venetian glass, cats eye, gemstones. If Christian hadn't been with me, I probably would have turned on my heels in ten minutes, overwhelmed and empty handed. He made it fun, arranging different styles and shapes on the counter, seeing which colors and textures complimented each other. "Christian, I can't thank you enough. I don't think I could do this without you."

"You don't need to thank me. This is a blast!" He held up sky blue faceted ovals, "These are fantastic, Cate! You have to use these."

I added a few strands of those to my basket and went to the checkout counter with enough to decorate at least thirty hats. As the woman rang them up, I watched the growing total, swallowing hard as I reminded myself to relax. Two hundred and eighty dollars later, we left the store. "Do you have to go to the gym?" I asked. "Can't you go tomorrow instead?"

"I'm sorry. I have to go. I didn't go yesterday, and I have class and work tomorrow."

I dangled the carrot, the hip bar with incredible sushi, "Are you sure? I'm going to Happy Fingers, right down the road." Slight guilt, at my attempt to be a bad influence nagged at me. "If you change your mind, that's where I'll be, but I understand. Those biceps won't define themselves." He hesitated, like he might change his mind, before saying that we would have drinks another time.

As soon as I sat down at the bar I got a text from Christian, 'The devil wears Betsey Johnson. Damn near impossible to get into my workout now.' My sake set down in front of me, I opened my newly purchased book on beading. I had just gotten through the intro when I felt a hand on my back and the presence of a tall man behind me.

A deep voice asked, "Interesting reading?" Thinking Christian had given into cocktails over the gym, I turned around smiling. My face fell when instead of Christian; the voice belonged to a guy who looked like the cuter Wayans brother.

"Oh no." I said, without trying to hide my disappointment. He was my worst nightmare, tall, handsome with a devilish grin.

"Can I buy you a drink?" he asked, slithering into the empty stool beside me. With a smirk on his face, he might as well have had on a shirt that said 'Cheating bastard who will charm you and squash you like a bug'.

Not caring that I was already over my budget I said, "No." and turned my head and tried to resume reading.

"Why not? What's the problem?" he asked. I felt myself growing angry. Did I have an asshole magnet in my pocket?

"The problem? I'll tell you what the problem is! Why can't you people get it through your heads?"

He stood up. "You people?" he asked, as if he didn't know exactly what kind of playboy he was.

"A girl can't sit here with a book without you thinking it's an invitation? Do I look like I'm trying to make conversation, like I'm not perfectly happy minding my own business? I know your kind, and I don't want any part of it."

His eyes narrowed, "My kind?"

"Yes, your kind." I sat up straight, proud of myself for calling him out on what undoubtedly was his well practiced routine. The old Cate would have been putty in his hands.

"You could have just said no thank you, you racist bitch." He started walking away. I sat there flabbergasted. Why the hell would he call me a racist? The exchange replayed quickly in my head. He was half way across the bar before I figured out what he was talking about.

"Wait!" I yelled. He didn't turn around, but slightly slowed his gait. I started to jump up, and the book I had put in my lap hit the floor with a loud thud.

I yelled, "I meant that you're a man!" He kept going, and as he walked further away, in a desperate attempt to redeem myself I yelled "I love black people! I do! Ask anybody, ask Oprah!" With that he was out the door, and I was left at the bar with a room full of people, all staring at me.

I went straight to Kay's. She wouldn't be home yet, but I couldn't bring myself to go home and face the emptiness of my condo. Besides, everything is better at Kay's: bigger place, better food, even her couch is more comfortable and she has a love seat too. I went inside and helped myself to the opened bottle of red she had out on the counter. I went to her back deck, figuring I would smoke and try to calm down until she got home. I opened the door to a loud shriek. Lainey was sitting there.

"Oh shit, Cate! You scared the bejesus out of me! What are you doing here?"

"Sorry, I…I just didn't want to go home. What are you doing here?"

Lainey smiled. "The same."

"Are you staying here?" It occurred to me that with her marriage ending she might have moved in with Kay.

"No, I just had to get out of the house. Everywhere I look there's pictures of me and Michael, smiling back at me, mocking me like I'm a big joke. I can't stand looking at them, anymore than I can suck it up and put them in boxes."

"If you want, I can come to your house and pack them up."

"Then what? Where do they go? I'm sure Michael doesn't want them…and I don't want to get rid of them. What do I do, take them with me and hide them in a closet?"

"Yes, that's exactly what you do."

"I don't even want to think about it right now."

"You don't have to. Want me to get you a glass?" I asked, holding my wine out.

"Yes, as a matter of fact I would. I was eyeballing that bottle earlier."

"What were you waiting for? You know Kay doesn't care. If she did, she would have known better than to give keys to us!"

"I was waiting for five o'clock. I don't want to turn into a wino."

"Oh please" I said as I got up and looked for Dean Martin's greatest hits CD. As soon as I found it I cued it to Little Ole Wine Drinker Me. "If it's good enough for Dean, it's good enough for me."

"At the rate things are going, I'm going to have to start drinking Vodka and Club Soda again. My ass is getting bigger by the minute."

"If you want to come with me, I'm going to start taking yoga. I figure the inner peace thing would be good, and I want the yoga body."

Lainey shook her head, "I'm not joining a gym. It's too depressing. Every time I've joined, I end up paying every month and not going."

"No, I mean real yoga. You read Eat, Pray, Love. I'm going to an ashram for the real deal."

"Uh uh, not me, Missy." Lainey was emphatically shaking her head. "I read Eat, Pray, Love but more importantly I saw Slumdog Millionaire. You won't catch me trekking across India to an ashram. That outhouse scene alone was enough for me."

"Have you lost your mind? They have ashrams everywhere, even in Atlanta. If I had enough money to go on some spiritual quest, I would already be long gone…and not to India, somewhere tropical."

"Ok, if you actually end up going, count me in for yoga. So what's new with you? Why don't *you* want to go home?"

I thought about my day, which even if it had started well, had gone to such shit that I couldn't bear to talk about it. "I don't want to talk about it. On a good note, I did get hats and beads to start a new business venture." I told Lainey about my plan to become a hat designer, and got the beads from the car to show her.

"Cate, I love this! This is such a good idea."

"You really think so? When we were at the beach, I almost asked you to go into business with me, but I didn't even have a plan yet."

"Thanks. That was a sweet thought, but I've got more than I can handle with the divorce. However, I know at least two people who have boutiques that would be perfect for selling these. I could put you in touch with them."

"Oh Lainey, that would be awesome!"

"That's what friends are for."

We were interrupted by Kay's voice, "Hey ladies! I didn't know I had company."

"Sorry," I said. "I should have called."

"Don't be sorry, it's a nice surprise. Impromptu parties are my favorite."

I held up the now empty bottle of wine. "I'm a bad guest. I showed up uninvited, empty-handed, and I drank your wine."

Kay smiled at us. "Drink all you want ladies. Andrew Firestone will make more."

When I got home, I had a voicemail from James. He said that he needed to see me soon, that he wanted to talk over drinks. Yes! I realized that I had been waiting for this call, the 'Cate, I can't live without you and want you back' call. He didn't have to say it, I knew.

I would tell him that it was no use, he couldn't win me back. I could see it coming. The flowers he didn't send after cheating on me would be arriving in a steady stream of big begging bouquets. I wanted to call everyone but knew they would just ruin it, telling me not to go, that I'm too good for him. It's not that I think I owe him any of my time, but to finally get the satisfaction of him wanting me is worth it. I wish I already had my yoga body. Maybe he will send flowers so I can justify meeting him, then a grand gesture that after a lot of wooing would make it ok to take him back. I might see him and feel nothing, but at least I'll get my dignity intact watching him try to win me back. I should pick a place with great lighting.

He once sent me roses with Grateful Dead lyrics on the card that read 'it must have been the roses, the roses or the ribbons in her long brown hair'. He loves my hair long and straight. I'll get it blown out before I meet him.

I called the salon. They could fit me in Friday afternoon. After confirming that it had been more than two hours since he left a message, I sent James a text. I was afraid he'd hear the eagerness in my voice if I called him back. Carefully worded to sound busy and casual, I sent "All booked up except Friday. If it's important could fit you in for happy hour. Andre's at 6?"

Immediate text back, "See you then." It wasn't bowling me over with his desperation, but I figured he would do enough groveling at Andre's.

Friday came quickly, although it killed me to keep it a secret. I went to Vivian's in the morning, leaving with dirt under my nails. When I got to the salon, the manicurist said she could fit me in for a manicure and pedicure. Budget be damned, this was important.

"Pick a color." She said. She looked like she couldn't have been a day older than twenty, with blonde hair on the top of her head, and black hair coming out of the bottom layers.

You first, I thought. I stared at the display, trying to tune out her chattering to her coworker as I looked at the shades of OPI nail polish. They were like a candy store for women. With names like 'Cha-ching cherry', 'Conga line-coral', and the classic 'I'm not really a waitress', I've always loved OPI polish. Picking up each dark color, I read the names as if there would be a magic message in the title of the perfect shade. Perhaps there was one named 'Life sucks without Cate'. I settled on 'We'll always have Paris'. It was the right color, even if it was the wrong mood.

As my feet settled into the hot foot-tub, she popped her gum and said, "So you're getting a blow out and a mani-pedi. You must have a big date!" I smiled but didn't say anything, hoping she would get the hint that I wasn't interested in a personal conversation. I wished I'd had time to go to my old nail salon, where it was half the price and the only conversation that wasn't in Vietnamese was when I was asked if I also wanted my nonexistent mustache waxed.

"If you ask me," she continued, "every woman should get dolled up for a night out, even if they don't have a date. I mean, when you're single it's even more important."

No one asked you, I thought, and wondered when I had become such a bitch. I closed my eyes, as if I was going to nap while the soles of my feet were scrubbed with what felt like a Brillo pad.

Three hours later I walked out of the salon, looking and feeling like a new woman. I couldn't get to Andre's first, so I drove around when his car wasn't there at six. Quarter past, his car was there. I parked and walked in, feeling like a bombshell.

My hair was perfectly smooth and straight, with a bump at the crown. I read once that men are genetically attracted to the bump, one of those primal things like how women give off different pheromones when ovulating. Instead of my standard American manicure, I went with the dark seductive shade on my nails and toes. You may not be able to buy happiness, but you can buy hotness. Wearing fitted jeans, a black cleavage baring top, and black strappy stilettos, I was as close as I could get to oozing sex appeal. He was at a table in the bar area. I leaned in to kiss him on the cheek, hoping he would drool at the smell of my new fragrance: Mystique.

"Thanks for coming." He said. I figured that was ok. It's not like he could drop to the floor immediately. I sat across from him, crossing my legs so he could admire my perfect vamp toes in to-die-for heels. *Casual,* I reminded myself.

"Well, here I am. I don't have a lot of time." I said, hoping he would go ahead and spill the 'I need you Cate' beans.

"You look great, by the way."

I tried to contain my smile, so he would know that his opinion didn't matter.

"Thanks." I said.

The waiter walked up and asked what I would like to drink. James used to always order a dirty martini for me, but he was obviously trying not to be presumptuous. He was probably glad he hadn't ordered me anything since I was clearly totally different than the person he knew six months ago. I thought about ordering a Manhattan or scotch, something different to match the new me. I couldn't think of anything fast enough, so I ordered my usual dry, dirty martini.

"How are you, Cate?" James asked.

"I'm great, fantastic really. I've started my own business, designing hats." It was almost true. I hadn't designed a single hat yet, but that was just because I needed to learn how to bead jewelry.

"That's great. Wow! I had no idea." He looked impressed.

"Why would you?" I asked, hoping to seem mysterious. "There are plenty of things you don't know about me, James. I've changed a lot since we were together." I tried to push my hair back over my shoulder, since a few stray strands were starting to stick to my lip gloss. I just missed flinging my hair into my martini that the waiter was bringing from behind me. He set it down, and I took a big sip.

"Yeah, that's what I wanted to talk to you about...change." This was the moment I had waited for. James was about to profess his love for me and say how amazing I was when we were together, that it was killing him to look at me now. He was going to tell me how much he's changed to become someone who deserves me. I sipped my martini, knowing it was better to act nonchalant and let him do the talking. "I wouldn't want you to hear it from somebody else. I'm getting married."

I sat there, wondering if he had noticed my sexy dark nails yet, as the words hit me like a ton of bricks. "What?" I asked.

"I'm getting married." He said again. "I thought you should hear it from me."

The room was getting smaller by the second. I took another sip of my martini, which was suddenly close to empty. I waved the waiter over, trying to focus on one thing at a time. First priority, I needed another martini. It was all I could do not to tell the waiter to 'Make it snappy!' I reached into my purse for a cigarette, relieved that Andre's still lets people smoke at the bar. I tried to steady my hand, not wanting James to see that I was trembling. "Married?" I asked, more than a little shocked.

"Married." James answered. Even with his British accent, all I could think of was Long Duck Dong from Sixteen Candles.

I smoked in silence until my martini arrived and James asked, "Cate, are you ok? I'm sorry. I knew this would be hard on you."

"This is not hard on me." I snapped. "I'm fine. When? Who is she?" I asked.

"Soon. We don't want to wait any longer." I cringed at the thought of him being a "we" with someone else. "It's Jessica, my boss."

My face grew hot. The only thing worse than James getting married was that he was going to marry *her*. She was supposed to be a mistake; the regrettable person who cost him his future with me. I could picture an old black and white film, where the woman throws a martini in some bastard's face before waltzing out of the room. It seemed like a good idea, but I didn't want to waste perfectly good Belvedere vodka, anymore than I trusted that my legs wouldn't wobble out from under me.

Don't cry, I thought, *say something sophisticated,* but my brain spat back at me with *douche bag*. In an attempt to buy time, I reached into my purse for my phone. He would see right through it, but I could say I felt it vibrate and fake a phone call. Either way, I needed a moment to regroup. With unexpected reprieve, I saw the picture of me and Christian from Niko's in my purse. Nimbly sliding it into my flip phone, as if it had fallen there, I grabbed my phone and quickly placed it on the table.

"Not to interrupt your fascinating story," I said as I flipped it open like I was checking my messages, letting the picture fall onto the table, "but my phone was vibrating."

I feigned casual distraction, pretending I hadn't noticed the picture. While I played a saved voicemail from Kay, I could see James out of the corner of my eye. He picked up the photo and looked at it.

As soon as I gathered my composure, I hung up and said, "Well if that's all you wanted to tell me, I should get going." I held out my hand for the picture. "Looks like I need to clean out my purse."

"Who's this guy?" James asked, but I couldn't tell if there was a trace of jealousy in his voice.

"Not that it's any of your business…" I said, sounding calm and collected. "Unlike you, I had the decency to wait until after you and I broke up to start dating. That guy is my boyfriend. Speaking of which, I need to go. He's waiting for me."

James nodded, "I'm happy for you, Cate." I wanted to scream at him, tell him that I was not happy for him, that I hoped the fleas of a thousand camels would infest his armpits. If I hadn't blown so much money on the pretense of my own magnificence, I might have gone off on him.

As it was, I had invested too much in this meeting to give up the ruse. I grabbed my purse and stood.

"Thanks for the drinks, James. Good luck! I'm sure Jessica's going to need it. When a man gives up his mistress, he creates a job opening." I smiled and walked to the door while resisting every urge to look back.

I drove straight to Jill's. The tears I expected to run down my face at any moment never came. When she opened the door she said, "I thought we were hanging out here. You're all dolled up for a night out."

"I was out." I said. "And now I'm here. I need a drink to tell the tale."

"Oh my…" Jill said, grabbing vodka from her freezer. "Martini?"

I nodded. "I've already had two, so I'm going to have to crash here. I need to borrow pajamas too. These jeans are going to cut off my circulation if I put another thing in my body."

I changed, and we went to her back deck so I could smoke. "I went out for drinks with James." I blurted it out like I was purging my sins in a confessional.

"You what? Why the hell would you do that?"

"You would be proud of me." I said, certain it was partially true. "I held my ground. I lied my ass off and told him Christian was my boyfriend, but I didn't fall to pieces or anything."

"Why did you go out with James?"

"He called and said he needed to see me."

Jill shook her head, clearly not amused by my lack of will power. "Curiosity killed the Cate." Unlike James, Jill noticed my manicure. "Oh my God, Cate, did you get your nails done for that piece of shit?"

"No," I answered. "I got my nails done for me, so I would feel put together...and I did. I kept it together even when he told me he's marrying his boss, Jessica." Then the tears came.

"Oh shit, Cate! I'm so sorry. No, he's fucking sorry. Oh God, I'm sorry too." She reached over to hug me. The tears stopped as abruptly as they started.

"Fuck him!" I said, "It's like in As Good As It Gets, when Jack Nicholson is crying after the guy comes and gets his dog. Then Jack starts laughing because he's crying and he says, 'Over a dog, over a damn dog.' James is a dog, and I'm not crying over him anymore."

"Good for you!" Jill said. "He doesn't deserve your tears, and he never did. I can't believe you didn't tell me you were going to meet him."

"I know, but you would've tried to talk me out of it. No matter how stupid it was, I had to go. I had to see what he wanted, and feel like I had the upper hand. Even though his news totally caught me off guard, for the first time since we broke up I got to feel good about how he sees me. I wasn't the girl throwing his shit off my balcony like a lunatic, I was composed."

"What's important is that you feel good about it. In a way, you got closure on your own terms, looking like a bombshell."

"I know! I was great, and left with my head held high. Even though tomorrow I know I'll think of ten brilliant things I should have said."

"Wouldn't it be great if we could press rewind and say exactly what we wish we had said? That would be the best super power, Re-confrontation Man, goes back in time and says all the things the rest of us think of after the fact."

"I did throw in that I wished Jessica luck, since when a man marries his mistress he creates a job opening."

Jill flinched. As soon as I said it, I felt bad. "Oh shit, Jill." I felt like I should apologize, but I didn't want to.

"Hey, it's true. My situation is my own damn fault. Don't sensor yourself because I've turned into a home wrecker. Steven and I are close to being done anyway." I wanted to believe her, but she'd said that before.

CHAPTER 9

Dear Oprah,

I am an emerging hat designer from Atlanta. My hats are beautiful and versatile, and worthy of a spot on your Favorite Things list. They have detachable jewelry, so you can dress them up or wear the jewelry separately. I'm an entrepreneur, a fearless female. I will send you one of my hats, so you can see the 'jewel' that they truly are.

Regards,

Cate

P.S. If you would like to order hats for you staff, please let me know.

A friend of Lainey's called me this morning about carrying my hats. Her name is Rita and she has a small boutique in upscale Buckhead, right beside Hermes! This is my big break, so I couldn't possibly tell her that I haven't made the hats yet. She wants to see them ASAP, before she leaves on a buying trip to New York. I need to make a prototype, but I can't learn how to bead jewelry in two days. Since Gorilla Glue has worked to repair everything from my broken reading glasses to my wedge sandals, I can use it to glue the beads onto a hat. I'll just wear a beaded necklace to show how the jewelry on the actual hats will be removable and able to be worn separately.

I had a lot to do in one day: going to Vivian's and coming home to establish myself as the leading designer in posh headwear. Even if I'm a big hat designer someday, I will still help Vivian. Going to her house is like a mini vacation for me, and I get to feel good about helping her. I thought Vivian would be reluctant to accept my free watering services in addition to my ten paid hours a week, but to my surprise she didn't hesitate.

As soon as I walked into Vivian's house, I could smell coffee and bacon. "In here!" she yelled. In the kitchen there was a plate of bacon drying on a paper towel, and a bowl of cut fruit.

"Are those mangos?" I asked.

"Breakfast of champions." Vivian smiled. "I don't care what anyone says, bacon is good for you. Fruit balances it out. What's new with you?"

"I am trying to design hats." As soon as I said it, I wished there was a little more confidence behind it. I felt like I might as well have said, I'm trying to reinvent the wheel.

"Well, honey, that sounds interesting. I didn't know you wanted to do that. Why don't you sit down and tell me about it?" Vivian moved the bacon and fruit to the table, which she had already set with dainty dishes befitting a tea party.

"I don't know if that's what I want to do, but I have to try something." I said, sitting at her kitchen table. "I don't know what's wrong with me. I'm thirty-two years old, and I'm still not sure about what to do with my life."

Vivian poured coffee for both of us. "That's how a lot of things feel at the beginning. You're out there trying things. Cate, I think you're brave."

I felt myself tearing up, and wondered when I became so emotional. "Really? I feel like a mess. I thought it would be so fun, so exciting, figuring it out. Instead I feel lost. I don't know why I still feel that way, when I have an idea about what I might want to do. Things are falling into place. I've bought the materials and have someone interested in selling the hats. Does it mean anything that I feel like a fraud, like I'm just flailing around pretending to be something, instead of becoming something?"

"What would it mean?"

"That I'm not on the right track. I feel like I don't know me anymore, like I've spent so long on a path that I didn't like, that I can't make it right. And when I'm here I feel like I'm trying to sponge off your life, soak up your happiness, your peace. I want what you have in your life for myself, and I don't know how to do that."

I let the tears fall only mildly worrying that Vivian would think I was a ridiculous, self-indulgent grown brat. Vivian left the room, returning with an embroidered handkerchief. She handed it to me. It was soft, like it had been washed a thousand times. As I dried my tears with it, she sat there looking at me with the tenderness of someone who would give anything to mend you if they could.

"It must be hard." Vivian said. "When I was your age, I was married, and I already had Betty. I know women's lib was supposed to do a world of good, and don't get me wrong, we needed equal rights, but no one told us how to do the rest of it."

"What? You don't think I'm pathetic, having every option and no idea what to make of them?"

Vivian shook her head. "Oh God, no. Your generation has all this pressure. You're supposed to have a successful job and be independent, but still find a good husband. You're supposed to have kids and be a good mother and spend the rest of your life juggling your so-called good fortune of having it all. I had the luxury of finding a hobby that I loved, without having to manipulate it into a career. I simply turned it into a business because I *wanted* to. Besides, back then there wasn't all this pressure to be happy."

"Vivian, do you think I'm silly?"

"Why would you ask me such a thing?"

"Is it silly that I can't even figure out what I love to try to make a living at it? I don't want to go back to nine to five, which is really eight to six, corporate life. I want to enjoy how I spend my days. I don't feel like that's asking for too much, but it's not happening very easily."

"The best things in life rarely happen easily." Vivian said before she took a bite of bacon. It was the thick cut slices that I love, but my anxiety had killed my appetite.

"I thought this would be different. I had felt like it was time for me to make a change before I got laid off. I even prayed for it, and I'm not religious. I thought it was kismet, the timing, that it would just work itself out."

"Maybe it is working itself out. Your idea of timing and divine timing may be very different things. How do you feel when you pray now?"

"Oh, I don't pray. That was sort of an isolated incident. I don't even go to church."

"I don't go to church either, but one doesn't have anything to do with the other. I pray when I'm working in the garden. It's the most spiritual thing I know."

"I'm not even sure how spiritual I am."

Vivian burst into laughter and continued for so long she sounded like she was trying to catch her breath. Buddy came over to the table, as if he was checking on her.

"Oh my," She said as she dabbed at her watery eyes, and started laughing all over again. It lasted so long, I started picking at a piece of bacon, wondering what was so funny.

"I needed that," she said when the second bought of laughter subsided. "What will they think of next?" Vivan shook her head and chuckled. "Trying to measure your spirituality is like trying to figure out how alive you are. You just are, and those two things are one in the same. If you're alive, you're spiritual by your very being. I'm sorry, honey, I hope I didn't hurt your feelings. I just got tickled..." She started laughing again.

"Picture…picturing you with a thermometer trying to see how much…" She waved her hand as she tried to quit laughing, tears streaming down her face. "Oh my, I'm sorry, I know this is important. I'm not trying to make fun, but when you get to be my age you have to take the laughs as they come." Vivian was still smiling ear to ear, wearing the remnants of her laughter. If I had known that my befuddlement would bring her so much amusement, I would have started confiding in her sooner.

"I'm glad to provide the entertainment, really."

"Seriously," Vivian said, still dabbing at her eyes. "Spirituality is within you. When you need guidance, ask for it. Even when you don't need guidance, keep the lines of communication open. It's important to feel connected, to be connected."

I wondered if this is why I didn't know which end was up, if I had let my request for guidance end with one prayer. I never set out to become a person of prayer; I just wanted to find my purpose in life. Before I could say as much to Vivian, I realized that the two are inseparably intertwined. Whether I wanted to or not, it was time for me to change. While it made sense that to change my life, I needed to change myself too, I had always resisted anything I perceived as religious in nature.

I couldn't ignore this fact any longer. A prayer had gotten me started on this journey, and it seemed that more prayer was my only way to continue. I hadn't defined my original prayer as anything more than what it was, a request for divine intervention. I just assumed that more prayer would have to be of a different nature, imagining myself with some nun-like devotion to something I don't completely understand, giving up all worldly desires and feelings. I thought that to be in tune with God, I would have to give up all the pieces that make me, me. Could the spiritually enlightened me still get excited about Chanel lip gloss, the annual Kate Spade sale, or even sex? I told Vivian my fears, as best as I could verbalize them, and asked her if there was hope for me.

She nodded in the direction of the back yard. "After breakfast, we'll start with the spring planting. Don't think about it, but when your mind settles, and you're not thinking about what to say anymore, start a conversation. Prayer is such a formal word. Let the garden be your sanctuary. I tell ya, honey, you're a product of Bible Belt living. God made you who you are. Now you have to give up the fire and brimstone version that you've inevitably had shoved down your throat and let God be God."

I ate a big bite of mango and contemplated this. Could it be that easy? Why not? It was when I prayed before.

Vivian set out packets of flower seeds and sent me off to a section of the garden to start. Sure enough, I got into a rhythm and the words came to me. Before I knew it, I was asking for guidance and direction. I didn't feel anything. A few hours later when all the seeds were planted, I felt a sense of calm, but no answer or gut instinct. I asked Vivian if that meant anything. She said the calm was my answer, that it was ok to try different things and see what stuck. I did feel inspired by the colors in the garden. Green was starting to appear on hydrangeas and hostas, with small but pretty buds of varying colors. Could that translate into the colors of the beads? My hat project didn't seem as stressful as it had at first. I could do this. It wasn't me hanging out on another limb. I was trying on different hats for my life.

When I got home, I went through the stack of mail that I had let accumulate into a pile on the kitchen counter. There were bills I hadn't expected. As I looked at my bank statement online, I saw that I was further over my budget than I had thought.

At the time I had bought my supplies, I rationed that is was necessary. You have to spend money to make money and invest in yourself. At the rate I was going, I would have to sort out my destiny fast. I tried to tell myself that this feeling was inevitable as my savings dwindled, but my sense of calm was dissipating fast and being replaced with the panic of before.

In an attempt to calm my nerves by focusing on the task at hand, I set out with a bottle of gorilla glue to create a prototype of my hats. After a lot of trial and error, I got the beads to stick to the wire. Before I knew it I had two hats, each with its own distinct flare, ready to bring to the meeting. The meeting went better than I could have imagined. The woman wanted to order thirty hats, only asking how quickly I could have them ready.

I tried not to chew on my lip as I wondered how quickly I could learn how to make the jewelry properly. As soon as I sorted out how to bead with the fish-line-like wire, I could work around the clock. I told her it would probably be a week. *There's no need to panic* I told myself, *Be grateful you have beads for thirty hats. So you are going to run out of money…and you're credit rating went into the toilet after some poor decisions in your mid twenties. You need capital, an investor.*

I decided to go to the credit union and apply for a loan. I'd done my banking there for ten years; surely it would pay off to have been a loyal customer all this time. I saw online that they had a program for new business owners and made an appointment. Dressed in my smartest suit, I went to my appointment with the downloaded paperwork already filled out.

After a lengthy wait, a small bald man with round rimless glasses came and sat down beside me. "Ms. Sanders, we appreciate your business, but your loan application has been denied."

I explained that I've been a loyal customer, and that my credit score was only low because after I bought my condo I bought furnishings that were no interest for 6 months, and then forgot all about it. By the time the bills came in, I thought they were promotional mailers, and I threw them away. I didn't even know I was on my way to credit hell until they started calling me. I was in my mid-twenties then and made some poor decisions. Couldn't we put up my condo as collateral? He paused, as if trying to be diplomatic before explaining that my mortgage was an interest-only loan, and the condo market had crashed with the rest of real estate. He said I had no equity in my home to use as collateral.

I went back to my history as a member of the credit union. He listened politely before telling me that my history with the credit union hadn't been desirable, and produced a list of all of my overdraft fees over the years. While trying to hang on to my last shred of dignity, I tried to explain to him that the overdraft fees were part of the profit they have made from having me as a customer. He said he was sorry, but that's not how the credit union views my history and that without any current sustainable income, I was too much of a risk. At that point there was nothing else to do. As if I had any money, an additional bank account that I had omitted from my application, I told him that I understood and would have to spend out of pocket.

It felt like a new low. I thought I was being proactive, applying for a loan before I was in dire need. Even with a little money in the bank, my own credit union wouldn't take a chance on me. As I sat in my car, I realized that I could scale back on transportation cost. I could trade in my BMW for a Honda, at least get my monthly payment down. If it came down to it, I would.

In the meantime, my car symbolized my own confidence in myself. I had worked my ass off to have a nice car that I enjoyed sitting in. With all the time I spent in Atlanta traffic, I had earned and deserved to have a car that I enjoyed, never mind the top of the line safety features that it probably has. Even though it's a depreciating asset, I had viewed it as what it was, the place where I spent more time awake than in my own home. I was not defeated, so there was no reason to downgrade yet.

CHAPTER 10

Dear Oprah,

You know one of the traits you and I have in common? I hate waste. I mean hate it. It makes me cringe. That's me with the skinny spatula, making sure I get the last sandwich's worth out of the peanut butter jar. Also me - trying to make sure the last paper towel on the roll, the one that has a little adhesive on it, gets used for something like a spill on the floor. You can't wipe glass down with those since it will smear.

It makes me sick to see something thrown away that could have been used or donated, anything with some life left in it. This deeply instilled belief of the importance and responsibility of fully utilizing what we have is also a source of shame for me now. If you look at my life right now, I can't find any gift that I have, any special talent or ability. And I know it's there, because I'm here and God doesn't waste.

Regards,

Cate

P.S. When you had the guy from The Marriage Ref on your show, I know you were about to die when they showed the clip of the guy who wouldn't use the last of anything. I was right there with you.

While I had been discovering that I wasn't credit worthy, Christian had sent me a text asking if I could meet for sushi and sake. As much as I wanted to duck my head into the sand and pretend that my financial situation wasn't dim, I couldn't keep ignoring it. I did the smart thing and invited him over to my place. He accepted. I smiled to myself, my new "boyfriend" was going to see me in my own habitat.

He got there right as I was pulling into the parking lot. "So this is where you hang your pretty hats!" He said as he walked into my condo, giving me a nod of approval. "This is so you," he said, "classic but with a certain flare. And the plants look good in here."

I noticed him moving them around and realized the difference between direct and indirect light. Christian made me feel good about myself, in a way that I hadn't felt in a long time.

"Glad you like it; especially since all that I've put into this place has made me unworthy for a business loan." His face reflected concern that I didn't want to deal with. "It's fine, really. I'm just so glad you're here. Want red or white?" I asked, holding up two bottles of wine.

"Red's good." He answered. I poured two glasses and steered him to my smoking area, the balcony. "So I want to hear all about the hats."

"It's going great!" I answered, wondering if I could say it enough to make it true. "That's not true. I don't know what the hell I'm doing. The good news is that someone's interested in buying them; the bad news is that I still have to figure out how to design the jewelry. I haven't even started reading the 'how-to' book yet…which isn't like me. Back when I had a real job, I never would have procrastinated like this. Now that I don't know what to do, and I don't trust my instincts, I go between completely frozen and whirling dervish mode."

"Why?"

"Um, why? I don't know why. If I knew why, maybe I could fix it."

"Then aren't you trying to figure out why?" Christian may have missed his calling as a therapist.

"Well, no. I figured that things would fall into place, and they're not. So now I'm wondering if I'm not doing the right things because *this* isn't the right thing. Jill, my best friend, loves her job. She may complain about it, but she loves it. Even when she's complaining about it, you can tell she's happy with what she's doing, which is hard to pull off unless you really like what you do. My sister Kay is a teacher, which is what she has always wanted to do. When we were little, Kay made me play "school" all the time so she could be the teacher. If you get her talking about the new electronic boards, and her affinity for chalk…It's unmistakable that she feels so connected to what she's doing that she's nostalgic about how it was when she started. And don't pretend that you don't love your job. If you didn't, you wouldn't go back to school to become an expert. It feels like everyone around me knows their place in the world, except for me. Frankly I'm too old to not know."

"I think you're making this bigger than it is. Sounds to me like you're just overwhelmed, so why don't you break it down and do one thing at a time?"

God, I've missed man logic.

We finished a bottle of wine, and by the time we were done, I felt like everything was going to be alright. Christian offered to help me figure out the beading. I explained that I would feel like I couldn't call it my own if I had help. He reasoned that it was like helping me hook up a new stereo system. I decided to take him up on it, promising to pay him if and when I became a success. He humored me by saying that if I was a huge success I could pick up our future sushi tabs.

Feeling relief that I wouldn't be struggling through the book on my own, which had begun to seem as complex as a manual for a car engine in my mind, I decided to tell him about his new status as my "boyfriend".

"So enough about me, how are things going with the gayness?"

Christian almost spewed wine. "What?"

"Oh, I was wondering if you're still gay. I saw James last week, the piece of shit ex fiancé. Can we skip a long story, and leave it where he saw the picture of us at Niko's and I told him you're my boyfriend?" Christian laughed while he nodded consent.

"I panicked, and then I saw the picture of me with you, a hot guy." More than a little grateful that he thought it was funny, I gave him the shortest version possible, but owned up to my salon visit. "I didn't mean to use you." I said. "I had a weak moment."

"Use me! If I'm the hot guy, I'm flattered to be of service." We drank more wine, and I could almost forget that he is indeed gay. Luckily he left before I got drunk, saying he needed to get some sleep. Two more glasses of wine and I would have wanted to kiss him.

I've let my mail pile up again, basically because I've figured out that there is no good news coming to my mailbox. It is filled with catalogues for things I want but can't afford, and worse, bills I don't want and can't afford.

Knowing that watching it accumulate on the counter wasn't making it any better, I went through it. COBRA health insurance bill, car insurance bill, car payment bill, bills, bills, and more bills accompany my monthly bank statement. The only thing I wasn't expectantly dreading is the letter from my mom. It's about the weather, the outfit she got for sixty percent off, health updates on random people. There's also an article she cut out from Guideposts.

This is how my mother parents me. It works well for us and we get to skip long drawn out mother-daughter talks. Like the time in college when I looked up herpes, after a friend had a scare after a one night stand. My mom was a nurse, and there were always volumes of medical encyclopedias at our house. I mistakenly left a bookmark on the herpes page. She never mentioned it, but over the next few months she sent me safe-sex brochures and information on herpes medications.

Apparently Kay has told Mom about my dilemma, even though I would prefer that neither of my parents know that I'm a screw up. She has told me so many stories about her friends who have children moving back home after they lose their jobs or get divorced. Each time she shakes her head, and I can imagine how grateful she is that although Kay and I are still single, we aren't running back to their house in search of relief from the rest of life. Well, not yet anyway.

The Sister Schubert article in Guideposts read:

My future should have been clear to me from the start.

Then my marriage ended. At 40, I found myself a single mom of two girls, and I worried my income from working at Daddy's store wasn't enough to support them. I felt so alone.

"God, I can't do this on my own," I prayed. "I'm in your hands now."

The answer came back: Trust me, Sister. There's one thing you love doing more than anything else. Do that. I knew he meant Gommey's rolls. Could I really make a living out of them?

I know my mom sent this to be helpful, but instead of providing me any reassurance about what I'm doing, it makes me want to go to Vivian's. Perhaps my true calling is to be an emotional escape artist. Who would pay to watch me proverbially bury me head in the sand?

Even though I'm not supposed to go until tomorrow, I call Vivian to see if I can come over, not making any excuses for a reason. And she says, "Of course you can."

Whenever I ask her any mundane thing, 'can I have a cup of coffee, a recipe, can I borrow your lighter', Vivian always answers with 'of course you can'. Every time she says it, the words wrap around me like a blanket. I wished this is how my prayers worked. I would ask God, 'Can I be a happy, successful hat designer?', and He would send the message right back, 'Of course you can.'

When I walk in the door, I breathe in the smell of coffee and wish I lived with Vivian. Perhaps it's because I have switched from the good coffee which was ten dollars a pound, to something that comes in a big plastic bin, two pounds for five dollars.

"Perfect timing," Vivian says, as she pours two cups, "It's time for a smoke break."

As I step out onto her back deck the feel of cool morning air mixed with sunshine hits my face, something that never happens on my balcony. Vivian's engraved silver lighter is on the table. When I have money, I want to get one of my own.

I stare into the garden, amazed at how there is always something growing, something about to sprout, something at the end of its harvest yield. Vivian told me that spring is her favorite time of the year for the garden, but I can't imagine it getting any better than this. "Where's Buddy?" I ask, missing the feel of his wet nose on my elbow that usually accompanies every smoke break.

"Buddy has earned himself a bath, chased a squirrel straight through the mud. He's too big for me to do it myself, so he's got a day at the groomers."

"I could have bathed him."

"No, honey. That is a job worth paying an expert, or at least someone with a proper dog tub. It's not worth the mess." Vivian takes a sip of her coffee and a drag of her cigarette. She too is staring into the garden as she says, "You know, I thought of you this morning when I was dropping him off. Buddy's been going there since he was a puppy. It's a small place. Two ladies own it, nice as they can be. You can tell they really love the dogs, that it's not just a business to them, it's personal. They're doing something that they care about. I'd never given it any thought before, but today I thought of you." Vivian gives me a small wink, and I notice how her eyes, corn flower blue, are so vibrant that her skin never looks washed out against her white hair.

"You get one life." She continued. "I used to be disappointed that Betty didn't want to take over here when I retire, but this isn't her dream. To tell you the truth, I don't think being a florist is either. People say life is short, and sometimes it feels that way. One thing I know for sure, sometimes it's long too."

When we finished our coffee I offered to help Vivian in the garden. "There's nothing that has to be done today." She answered. "I've cut back a little bit. They say eighty's the new seventy, but I don't have the energy I used to. Since you're here though, why don't I take you through the greenhouse?"

I followed Vivian through the back garden, excited to see something new. "I feel bad, monopolizing your time when I'm not helping." Besides that, I enjoyed losing myself in the rhythm of planting and watering.

"You're not monopolizing my time. You know I used to hear my friends bragging about their grandchildren and wish that I had them, but Betty never wanted kids. Then I'd hear people complaining that their grandkids didn't want to spend time with them, talking about how they only saw them at holidays or when they felt guilty about not visiting. My point is, you coming over here just because you want to spend time with me is more than a compliment. It makes me feel special."

As soon as she said it, I knew that the fact that I made Vivian feel special might be one of the greatest compliments of my life.

When we got to the greenhouse door, I was stunned by how big it was. With all of the dogwood trees in the back of the yard, you couldn't see half of it from Vivian's deck. It was bigger than my condo. As Vivian opened the door, I could feel my hair starting to frizz from the humidity. It was like walking into some exotic jungle, right in the middle of Atlanta. The first thing that caught my eye was a huge round table covered with potted orchids. They were so pretty and so delicate, I felt like a lumberjack beside them.

"You don't have to grow orchids in pots. I especially like them mounted on wood, but those don't sell as well in Betty's shop. Come on back," Vivian said as she walked around the table. The greenhouse was one big room, but she has sectioned areas off with the plants. There were ferns everywhere, stacked on shelves like a display. We walked past them and I saw rows of huge pots, filled with plants that had long green draping leaves.

"What are these?"

"Those are Agapanthus, Lily of the Nile. They're evergreens, but they grow best when they're crowded, so I always keep a bunch in pots back here. You should see them bloom. There will be huge stalks on these that open up into a big, pale blue flower. I think they'll make your jaw drop more than the orchids. I cut them and Betty uses them as the center flower in her big pieces. That's something you don't see everyday."

As I followed her to the back, I was expecting something magnificent, something worth hurrying me past the orchids. But Vivian stopped at a table in the back with rows of little brown pods with tiny bits of green poking through. Vivian took a deep breath and smiled. I tried to muster up some enthusiasm, but it was basically little clumps of dirt wrapped in netting. "I don't get it." I said.

Vivian didn't seem disappointed. "You will." She said. "These are moonvines, and they are the show stopper of my garden come summer."

When I got home there was no use putting it off any longer. As much as I wanted to wait till I had Christian there as a reinforcement, I started reading the book on beading. As I read the same page over and over again, too bored to focus, I tried to remind myself that it would be fun when I started beading. I found myself looking for a distraction, laundry to put in the wash, anything else to do instead. Overwhelmed by looking at the bag of beads beside me, I tried to figure out what Oprah would do. She would do this bead by bead.

Two hours later, I have finally made progress. I don't know when I turned into this person who can't get it together.

That's the thing about losing your direction. When it's hard to figure out where to go, it's always easier to be still. I can't afford to be still. Sometimes when I'm still I find myself wondering what my life would be like if I was married to James. And whenever I slide down that slope I picture me being married to the person I thought he was, not the person he turned out to be.

Either way, I've gotten through the basics of threading and knotting. I want to call it a day having reached my goal to finish the first two chapters of what feels like monotonous homework. Luckily I'm saved by the bell. Kay texts me when the school day ends. She's on her way over. As I put two martini glasses in the freezer to chill, I wish that this could be my life: tootling around and being social. Maybe it will be, when I'm "Out of the strain of the doing, into the peace of the done." as Julia Louise Woodruff put it.

By the time Kay arrives my condo is perfectly readied for company. My plants are still alive and everything, even the mail, is in its place. My home has never been so organized because now I welcome the distraction of made up tasks. I have gone through my closets and gotten rid of all old clothing, using Oprah's clutter experts advice of getting rid of everything that you don't need, use, or want. I have to confess, I have held on to a pair of size six jeans that I doubt my size twelve ass will ever fit into again. I know that if I ever get back to the weight of my early twenties, I will want new jeans. But getting rid of my once favorite denim feels like giving up on the possibility that my body will ever look like that again.

"What smells so good?" Kay asks.

"That would be the candles." I had fancy candles that I was waiting to burn or use for a gift when I needed one on short notice. After I found one beginning to melt in the closet, I'm no longer trying to save them for special occasions. Maybe it's better to redefine what special is. Because no matter how often Kay comes over, it should always be treated as special anyway.

Today the scent of lavender and vanilla is especially appropriate since Kay and I are having an at-home spa evening. In need of some cosmetic maintenance, it seemed the perfect idea when I found baskets full of sample size products while cleaning out my bathroom closet. I've gotten out my foot spa for our pedicures, and the products are displayed on the coffee table, organized by body parts. While I shake the martinis, Kay starts going through them. "How are we going to do this?" Kay asks.

"I figure we should wash our hair in the sink first. I've got a tea tree scalp shampoo and deep conditioning treatments. There are two slightly damp towels in the dryer. I'll turn it on, so they'll be warm. We can wrap those around our heads to let the conditioner soak in while we do our toes." Kay nods. I can tell she's surprised that I've thought this out. Normally I come up with a plan, and she has to work out the logistics since there's always something big that I've overlooked.

Even though we splash water all over my bathroom floor, we have sufficiently revitalized scalps according to the label on the shampoo packet. Wrapped in warm towels, our hair is hopefully being fortified with deep conditioner. We even delay our martinis to steam our faces over bowls of hot water with something labeled 'purifying facial sauna' soaking in it, although it looks like a bunch of crushed leaves and smells like rosemary. It says it will open pores and release impurities, but mainly I'm aware of how uncomfortable it is to bend my neck over the bowl. After the allotted three minutes of our facial steam, we debate whether it's worth it to put the purifying mask on our faces before we go on the balcony to smoke.

Finally Kay says, "We're going to smoke regardless. This either helps or it doesn't."

We sit on my balcony with the mint green mask on, smoking and sipping our drinks. I'm making a list of what to do next. Unlike my other to-do lists, with things like 'pick up dry cleaning' and 'sort out your future', this is fun to me, and will actually get done in a timely manner.

"Pedicure, manicure, eye treatment cream." I read them aloud. The towel on Kay's head begins to flop over, weighed down by the wet hair conditioning underneath.

As she straightens it, Kay asks me, "Do you ever get tired of this stuff? Wonder what the point is?"

I don't have to think about this. "Nope, I know what the point is. Deep conditioner works. My hair is going to look good all week."

"Not that," she says, again repositioning her towel, "All of it. The deep hair conditioner lasts for one week. You don't do it, and then it's done. It's constant maintenance."

"I like this stuff. It smells good. It feels good, and even the things that I don't see immediate results from, I feel proactive when I use them." It's true. I don't do these things, like the anti-aging treatments, out of fear of what will happen if I don't use them. I enjoy them. I'm a girly girl, and I like that I smell like one, that my skin is soft from exfoliating regularly in the shower, and moisturizing after. I wish the anti-cellulite creams worked, but that would be a miracle.

"I thought you wanted to do this." I say, as it occurs to me that Kay isn't enjoying this.

"No, I do. I'm having fun with you. I didn't mean it like that. It just pisses me off a little bit that there's an expectation to do all of this. Like tonight, we're just doing part of the maintenance. I still need to use my teeth bleaching kit again, get my hair cut and colored, a keratin treatment, my brows threaded, and a bikini wax. All this on top of the stuff I do almost every day, like shaving my legs and styling my hair."

"Well if you don't have money for laser hair removal or want to be hairy, you have to shave." I try not to envy Kay. Lately I've wanted to go to the salon with the same intensity of a chocolate craving when I have PMS.

Kay shook her head, causing the towel to fall forward again. "I don't even mind doing this stuff. I'm used to it. It's just that here I am, doing all of this stuff all the time, and it's unfair. Because this is the truth; tomorrow I could meet an overweight man, with a bald head and excess hair everywhere else. As long as he's smart, employed, makes me laugh and feel special, he's met the basic criteria of what he needs for me to find him attractive. For me to get that same man's attention, I have to do all of this," she motions with her pointer finger from the towel on her head to her toes which are fanned out with purple foam separators, "plus be smart, successful, and have a sparkling personality."

I thought about our couple friends and realized how true that really was. "That's kind of depressing." I said.

As if she was laying down a trump card, Kay added, "And that doesn't include summer, when we're getting our hair highlighted and trying to stay tan while using sun block."

"I take that back. That's really depressing." I drank the last sip of my martini. "I've lost my will to beautify. Do you want to skip the pedicures and just drink martinis?"

"Hell no." Kay answered, and then a grin spread across her face. "I need a pedicure. I have a date tomorrow night."

CHAPTER 11

Dear Oprah,

My friend Vivian has a banana tree. I was asking her why it's called a banana tree since it doesn't produce bananas. She said that the tree would produce bananas but where we live, the temperature isn't quite right. She digs it up every fall and stores it inside for the winter, replanting it every spring. The fact that this same tree in a different location would produce bananas, makes me wonder if that's how I am right now. And if I'm in the wrong place, how do I know where to go? Is it literally geography, or is it something within me?

Are you having the same struggle? You were on Keeping Up With the Kardashians. I'm not judging, but really, I don't think you would have done that a few years ago. I hope you're on the right path for you. No pressure, but I'm counting on you for some answers.

I'm ashamed of myself for not knowing what to do, and not trusting that my life is in God's hands. It feels conflicting to me though. I'm responsible for my life, for bringing what I want into fruition. Am I supposed to plug along even when I can't hear any guidance from above? Do I assume I'm on the right path? Part of me knows that I should be quiet and still and listening for the guidance, but for how long? Frankly, time is not on my side.

Regards,

Cates

P.S. Your hair looked so good on last night's Where Are They Now. I feel like I could use a change too.

Usually I delay starting each day by getting online. You can pass a lot of time on the internet, even when you're trying not to. It always puts a damper on my morning because it's a constant reminder that I was supposed to be married now. I still get emails from every wedding service imaginable, despite all of my efforts to unsubscribe. They taunt me with offers of personalized wedding favors, veil styles for every bride, and drawings for honeymoon packages. Grateful that I'm going to Vivian's today, I don't check my emails.

Whenever I walk into Vivian's house the smell is different, but always of something that makes my mouth water. Buddy comes to greet me before leading me back to the kitchen, his favorite room in the house. There are pies on the stove top and more on trivets on the counter, and some still in the oven. I can't pinpoint the smell. Vivian is milling around in her pantry, pulling out spices to hold them closer to the light. She reads the labels and puts them back.

"Perfect timing," She says to me. "For the life of me, I can't find the cinnamon." I start to walk toward the pantry, and notice the cinnamon is already on the counter.

"It's here." I answer, holding up the bottle.

"Well I declare. If it was a snake it would have bitten me." She laughs at herself and mixes the cinnamon into a bowl of sugar. Before I ask she answers, "Ladies Guild Bake Sale. This is for the apple pies. The rutabagas are already cooling."

"Rutabagas?" I know my grandmother used to make them, but I don't remember anything else about them.

"I don't know what the south is coming to when a southern girl doesn't know about rutabagas. Rutabagas are a root vegetable. These are from the garden, the very last of this season. They look like a turnip, but when you bake them with a lot of sugar…" I must be making a face because Vivian starts over. "Think of them like you would sweet potato pie. Trust me, they're good."

They must be good because she has made at least ten of them. She puts the cinnamon mixture on the apples with a scoop of butter on top before placing them in the oven. She sets the timer for an hour and says, "Let's get to gardening!"

Vivian has four big baskets full of bulbs. I hazard a guess, "Tulips?"

"No, you plant tulips in the fall, and that's probably why a lot of people think that's when you plant bulbs. Bulbs flower most of the year though, and spring is when you plant a lot of them, especially my favorites." There's a note card on each basket: canna lily, dahlia, gladiolus, and iris. I can picture all but the canna lily, so I ask Vivian what they look like.

"They're tall, grow anywhere from three to six feet. They have a stalk base, so not a popular cut flower. They come in different colors, but those are red. They will bloom all summer long, so I grow them just to enjoy here in the garden."

Vivian sets the bulbs in position, for me to follow behind and plant them while she finishes her pies. She tells me it's not that important where they go since they each have their own row, as long as they're spaced so that the roots have room to spread. She sees this as instinct because to her it is. I have a feeling that if she saw what my instinct would be, she wouldn't be encouraging me to trust it.

Buddy sits beside me, watching me dig each little hole like it's the most interesting thing he's seen, like he hasn't watched this over and over again his whole life. Every so often he licks my pants leg and looks away, sneaking in his kisses.

She asks me how my home spa evening went. I tell her Kay's theory on maintenance and men. Vivian doesn't slow down for a minute. She keeps placing the bulbs in the spaces that will become their new homes, all the while shaking her head.

"Women have been doing that forever." She says. My mind flashes to my last Brazilian wax. As if she can sense that I think I know something she doesn't, she shakes her head again. "You know, go back as far as you like…from the Asian women binding their feet, to not that long ago when women were wearing corsets and crushing their own ribs, women have been torturing themselves in ways that men would never consider. Times won't change…" Vivian moves to the next row. I'm waiting for her to say something prolific about how change will come when women need to set their own standards for beauty, when she starts speaking again. "…And anyone who tells you that times have changed probably needs a history lesson."

Two hours later I have planted all of the bulbs. As I wash my hands, coffee is brewing and Vivian is spooning baked apples into small bowls for us. It smells like Christmas. The apples are caramelized and tender, melting in my mouth. "I have a favor to ask you." Vivian says.

"You know how to pick your moments. Ask away." I think she is a genius. She could probably feed her baked apples to any threatening country and get them to give up their nuclear power plants.

"I'm going to the Women's Guild Annual Retreat after the bake sale. I was hoping you would stay here with Buddy. It's just two nights. Don't feel bad if you want to say no. Betty would do it, but frankly, Buddy would prefer you."

Elated, I could hardly wait the twenty four hours to start my weekend with Buddy.

When I got home I packed a bag, so excited to be staying at Vivian's. I need the bag by the door as a reminder that I'm leaving. It's not that I don't like my place, I do. I bought it as a single girl's condo with a five year plan. I got a great deal on it, and had figured that in five years I would have equity to turn it over and make a little profit. With my interest only loan this had seemed like such a smart idea, and cheaper than renting. With the market in deep decline, real estate jargon for the shithole, it is worth even less than I paid for it 6 years ago.

It's still a great condo for a single girl; small, near the nightlife, no yard to maintain, and neighbors who'd hear me scream if someone broke in. The problem is that I don't want single girl life anymore.

I'll wait for the right person. I don't want to be with someone for the sake of not being alone. But as far as I can see it's just me, and I'm tired of waiting for the house I want. Between the feeling that these walls are closing in on me and the loneliness that has sat on my chest since the break up, it's hard for me to be still here. The house I want matches the life I thought I'd have by now. The life I want includes a fireplace and room for a dog and twenty other things that don't fit into 700 square feet. Now that I'm tethered to my condo, I don't like being here.

It's not just me, these things happen to single women everywhere. If there were a Murphy's Law of Single Girl Real Estate it would be this: As soon as you buy a home you will meet Mr. Right and he will have a better house. It happened to Lainey. After she finally bought her cozy house she met the man she would marry. Then she spent the next year trying to unload her newly beloved home like it was a burden.

Telling myself that I can't make excuses and complain to myself about my condo, I decide to try the basic beading technique in chapter three. Like my own babysitter I have given myself permission to meet Jill at the pub after I complete three strands. I pray that it doesn't take long to do that, and remind myself that if I make a lot of money I can rent my place out and live somewhere else.

The wire for the beads is hard to bend. The book's illustrations shows adult hands, making these teeny tiny knots after each bead is on, but even with pliers I can't get it to work. My hands feel like they're two sizes too big, and half as strong as they need to be for this task. After two hours I have small puncture wounds on every finger, like pen dots where the wire has poked into me. I only have half a necklace done, but I don't give a shit.

There has to be a better way to do this, and I know I'm not going to figure it out tonight. Knowing I can't afford to go out, I invite Jill over for drinks.

"Let's go out." she says. As tempted as I am, one look at the bills on the counter and I have to tell her that going out isn't an option. "I've got it." She says. I know she means it, but I feel like a bad date. I don't know how many times she has said this since I got laid off, but if feels like too many.

Jill doesn't want to go to the pub, "Somewhere nice." she said, so I meet her at the wine bar Kay likes. When I get there I scan the bar looking for Jill, but don't see her until I notice her hand waving me over. Her hair, normally light brown and shoulder length is now a deep shade of chocolate level with her chin. Her face, always with such minimal, natural makeup that you can hardly tell she is wearing any, is now old

Hollywood glamour. Replacing the neutral toned suits that fill her work wardrobe is a black sheath dress. I sit and study, like I'm playing a game of photo hunt between this person and the Jill I know. She has black liquid eye liner, shimmery gold eye shadow, and dark red lipstick with a shine like glass. It's possible that she's wearing fake eyelashes.

If it were anyone else, I would be telling them how fabulous they look. But this is Jill, who has never worn this much makeup in her life, not even to prom or a costume party. "What's going on?" I ask.

"I just felt like something different." She says this like I don't know her, like I don't know that this is more than being in the mood for something different. Because I'm her friend, because the eye liner doesn't keep me from seeing that her eyes are sad, I let her get away with this for now.

We order wine. Even though they have beer, Jill says that she wants to share a bottle with me. She tells me about her work week. She's worked at the same office for so long that I know all of her office's gossip well enough to follow along like it's a reality show just for me. Despite the fact that normally this would be truly entertaining for me, it's hard to focus.

I get distracted by trying to decide whether she looks more like a mannequin or if with her hair slicked back, more like the girls in a Robert Palmer video. As I'm debating the difference between the two in my head, Jill says, "So, tomorrow's going to be a long day for me. How's it going with the hats?"

I shake my head in response, and instead tell her that I'm going to dog sit for Buddy. I tell her that Vivian and I sowed seeds for the herb garden, listing them off: dill, thyme, sage, marjoram, chives, lavender, and sweet basil. Surprised by my own excitement I tell Jill about how we also have a variety of mints, and that Vivian has put me in charge of them. I didn't know there were so many varieties, even a chocolate mint. I'm most excited about the pineapple mint.

Vivian can tell what everything is by looking at the plants, but she still uses plant markers because she likes the way they look. They're small posts that you stick in the ground, and they have a copper band at the top. You take a wooden skewer, using it like a pencil, and write on them, engraving the copper. I'm going to name the row of mint 'Mojito Avenue'.

The waitress comes over and refills our glasses, which aren't empty, from the bottle on the table. I hate it when they do that because I can't keep track of how much wine I've had.

Either I've bored Jill with what I thought was fascinating herb chit-chat, or she's finally ready to tell me what's really going on. Something different, my ass.

Finally she breaks the silence, "Steven and I are over."

"That's great!" I say this not only because married men shouldn't be dating, but because this cheating asshole would no longer be keeping her from finding someone worthwhile. As soon as the words leave my lips I see her face fall. There isn't a physical transformation strong enough to overpower the visibility of her disappointment. I hear Lainey in my head reminding me that when you're heartbroken, how it's broken doesn't make it less or more. Pain is pain.

"I'm sorry. I don't know what to say. I didn't know…" My voice trails off as I realize all that I didn't know. I didn't know that she cared about him so much, that she wasn't always prepared for this to end, or that it would hurt deeply when it did. All she had said was that she knew he was never going to leave his wife, and I had assumed everything else.

"I wish I could tell you what you want to hear, that my guilt overcame me at Mass one Sunday and I came to my senses. The truth is that he lost interest in me..." I light a cigarette and listen. "And I feel like shit. And I don't even get to feel sorry for myself because I deserve this."

I always thought that what she deserved was a man of her own. The whole time she was with him I wondered if she knew that, or if she was with him because she thought she deserved less. Now I wonder if she believes she deserves to feel like shit because she was involved with a married man, or if she always felt that way and that was why she dated one. Either way, I know why she goes to mass every week. Jill is looking for redemption.

Jill nods at my cigarettes on the table. "Give me one of those."

Without giving it a thought I say, "No, they're bad for you." Jill has never smoked anything in her entire life. If she's going to start now, she will have to do what most of us did with our first cigarette, take it without permission.

Jill has basically looked the same since she was in high school, so I already know the answer before I ask. "So which came first, the breakup or the makeover?"

"It wasn't exactly a breakup per se, but it's clearly over."

"How does that happen?"

"I just know. Between his marriage and my work schedule, we have to plan to see each other, designated times to talk on the phone…it's a lot of effort. Lately he hasn't called when he normally does. He says he's been really busy at work, which is complete bullshit."

The waitress comes by to see if we want another bottle of wine. We answer "yes" in unison.

"This whole time he has been pursuing me, always eager to find a time when he can arrange to see me. I haven't seen him in a month. And the last time I saw him, he came late and left early."

"That's what makes you think he lost interest?" I ask. Not that I think she should stay with him regardless, but it doesn't sound that clear cut to me.

"No, but he has, for sure. He didn't make a plan to see me, so I asked him what his schedule looked like. He said this month is going to be really hectic. I know it's over."

"Here's to moving on." I hold up my glass to clink hers. "Why don't we get drunk tonight? Maybe go out dancing or something? In case you forgot, that's going out makeup you're wearing."

"Oh, this. Yeah, I went shopping after my hair appointment, and the girl at the MAC counter did this." That explained a lot. I had wondered how she had learned to apply makeup with the precision of a geisha overnight. "I can't. Remember, I have that big meeting tomorrow?"

"Call in sick."

"No, I should be there. After this bottle, it's bed time for me." As if it was a sad and unfortunate thing, I wondered when Jill had become such a grownup.

CHAPTER 12

Dear Oprah,

Things are off to slow start. So I am trying to be proactive, practice gratitude, and focus on the positive. I wonder if you would approve and call this part of my journey.

When you called Dr. Phil to help you with the cattle mess in Texas, you must have felt the way I do now. You needed some oomph on your side. You knew who to call and had the money to hire the kind of support you needed. I am so glad you have had the support you have needed.

I am beginning to feel like I need more solid support. I've started getting panicky with every bill that comes in the mail. I have given it a lot of thought, and I don't know what you would do in my shoes. I think you would keep plugging away. So that's what I'm going to do. Plug away and keep writing to you.

I'm grateful for what I have and the people in my life. I really am. I would still like it if you and I could hang out sometime.

Regards,

Cate

P.S. I know you're not trying to hang out with me. I just thought I would throw it out there in case you are having one of your wand brandishing moments and decided to grant a wish.

The next morning I pull into Vivian's driveway to find her putting her weekend bag into the front seat of her truck. I would have done this for her, but know better than to tell her that I wish she'd left this for me. She's wearing loose black pants and a bright floral shirt. I've never seen her in anything but her gardening clothes, and I'd assumed that's what she always wears. She smiles and waves so big you would think she was trying to flag me down.

I return the smile and wave. "You look nice!"

She's practically glowing. "Do you like my shoes?" She kicks one of her feet at me. "They're new!" She's wearing black mary jane's. I have a pair just like them, if you don't count the 4 inch heel on mine.

"I love them!"

"Come on inside," she says. "I need to show you where everything is so I can hit the road."

"Sounds like you're looking forward to it." I said, somewhat surprised. A weekend retreat with the Ladies Guild seemed to me like something Vivian would only do to appease Betty.

"I am. When I was younger I thought this stuff was so silly, the sort of things that women do when they don't have real friends. I guess now that this is the only girls' weekend away I have, I'm not quite as fussy as I used to be."

I want to tell her that I think it sounds like a lot of fun, but Vivian's bullshit meter is stronger than I am daring, so I'm not going to test it.

She walks me back to the pantry, showing me the large bin that holds Buddy's food.

"Just fill up his bowl whenever it gets low." She opens her refrigerator. "Help yourself to anything." She says, and points at a covered Corning Ware dish. "Since you won't let me pay you, I figured the least I could do was make my favorite chicken casserole for you."

She had offered to pay me to stay with Buddy, but I couldn't take her money. As badly as I need money right now, my time is the only thing I have to give Vivian. I want to reciprocate her kindness, and this small favor is all I can afford. I don't even feel right about calling it a favor, knowing how much I want to be here.

"You said your apartment is too small for entertaining, so I thought you may want to have your friends over here while I'm gone. There's a wine rack in the bottom of the liquor cabinet. Make yourself at home."

There's an old trunk open in the living room, which looks like its contents have recently been rummaged through. It looks heavy, and I wonder where it was before and hope that she didn't drag it out herself. She sees me looking at it.

"Those are just some old clothes and things I've saved. There's going to be a fashion show at the retreat.

I thought some of my old dresses would be fun, but they didn't hold up very well." She picks up one of the dresses, layers of mint green chiffon under a gold satin bodice. It's beautiful, striking really, but the chiffon is starting to fall apart. I can see tears in the darting.

"It's gorgeous. Do you want me see if I can get it mended?" I ask.

"No, honey, unless you want it, but I don't think it's worth the trouble. That dress had its heyday a long time ago. I've taken everything I want from that trunk, but I left it out to see if you wanted it. You said you don't have a lot of room in your place, and I thought you could put the trunk at the end of your bed, maybe store your winter sweaters in it or something."

"I would love it."

"Great! When I get back, you can use the truck to take it home. Trash bags are under the sink. Unless you want something in it, you can just throw it all away. My flapper dress was still in mint condition, so I have all I needed." Vivian squats down and says good bye to Buddy, "Have fun!" she says to me with a wink, and she's out the door.

Unlike the deafening silence of my home, the quiet of Vivian's is soothing. I wish I could pack the peace into the trunk and take it home with me. Taking a cue from Buddy, who is laying on the floor beside the trunk, I sit down and pick through its contents. In addition to a few other dresses, worse for the lack of wear or time, there are rolls of fabric wrapped around cardboard. One roll is light blue chiffon, only different from the mint green fabric of the dress in color.

From where I'm sitting on the floor, I can see how the baseboards are ever so slightly uneven. Vivian's words come back to me, "There's something beautiful about the imperfections of an old house." I see the irregularities in the old hardwood and know exactly what she meant. Vivian told me to feel free to invite people over, and I would like to share this with friends, but don't know who to call.

I feel like I've worn Jill out with my neediness, and Kay too. Even when I'm working hard to keep the conversation away from the chaos that has become my life, it's still there. It sits between us like an elephant in the room because I have no good news to share, nothing to contribute.

Everyone has different levels of friends, the ones closest to you and then the people on the fringe who you know only bits and pieces of their business and vice versa. If you ever doubt who your fringe people are, lose your going out money and you will find out. These are the people who need an outing, who don't care to see you enough to sit at each other's houses and talk over a bottle of wine. They need entertainment, and you're not enough.

My fringe friends quit calling after the blue cheese debacle. Worse than that, I realized that my old friend Emma has become a fringe friend. I texted her one night about getting together, and she replied that she was sick. The next day I noticed her Facebook status, Comments made it clear that not only had she not been sick, she had been bar hopping. When you don't even merit concealing a lie on Facebook, you quickly feel like a loser. It's the internet equivalent to high school, finding out that you weren't invited to the big party.

The reminder of this is enough to send me into action, inviting Jill, Kay, and Lainey over for a girls' night. This is the perfect setting for a night spent sipping wine on the deck. Vivian has beautiful antique wine glasses, nothing resembling the plain stemless glasses at my house, which I thought were sophisticated when I bought them. These glasses have flowers etched into the base of the glass, and feel delicately thin on my lips.

By the time they get there, the smell of Vivian's casserole in the oven has taken over the house. I have cut flowers from the garden, just enough to fill her equally delicate bud vases. It doesn't take much to make the house feel enchanted.

While Kay and Jill look at the odds and ends of collections I've never noticed, Vivian's pictures and spoons from places that she visited hanging on a rack on the kitchen wall, Lainey and I pour the wine. "Show me the garden." Lainey says.

We step out the glass doors to the back, Buddy following us. I've turned on the white twinkle lights that Vivian has around the railing of the deck. Lainey takes a deep breath, "This is incredible." With a stride longer than mine, she reaches the garden ahead of me, stopping to pick a sprig from one of the many rosemary plants that Vivian has in pots by the arched trellis at the entrance of the garden. Lainey bends it in her fingers, smelling it. "By your garden gate…" She says.

"I wish Vivian was here," I say. "She could tell you what everything is."

"You don't have to know anything about this garden to appreciate it. This is a labor of love." I feel as proud as if it were my very own.

One chicken casserole and three bottles of wine later, we are all sitting on the back deck. Vivian's depression era glass ashtray is on the table. Vivian took her lighter with her. I can imagine her at the retreat, sneaking a cigarette like a rebel teenager at a youth camp. Lainey says, "I love it here. Cate, I would hide out here too if I could, especially now that the divorce is getting ugly." I'm exposed. I didn't realize that anyone else was aware that I had been doing anything more than helping in the garden.

"What do you mean?" Kay asks. "I thought you said Michael was being fair."

"He was," Lainey answers. "At least I thought he was, but then the divorce attorney told me I wasn't seeing things clearly. He brought up what I lost by selling my house, and how much Michael makes, that he's a public figure and wouldn't want any embarrassment. I didn't know how mad I was until then. Now our marriage has been reduced to rumors of infidelity."

I had never thought of a sports caster as a public figure, but I guess in that world he is. "They're saying that you cheated on him?" I ask.

"What rumor?" Kay asks before she can answer me. This is so big; I can't believe Lainey hasn't told Kay before now.

"That he cheated on me. They said if it got into the papers it would speed things up."

"But he didn't cheat on you." I said. "Why would he say that he did?"

Jill sips her wine, and then stares into her glass, as if she's inspecting it for a gnat.

"He didn't." Kay says shaking her head as she stands and walks into the house.

Lainey lights a cigarette. "But then how?" I ask.

"I did it." I look at Jill, then back at her, confused. "Cate, I started the rumor."

We sit in silence, and it becomes clear that Kay isn't come back anytime soon.

"I think I'm going to call it a night." Jill says before going inside.

"I should be the one to go. I've ruined the evening." We both know that Lainey's not going anywhere. Unlike Jill, the rest of us haven't been slow sipping our wine.

We hear Jill's car start in the driveway. Lainey says, "I knew it was wrong," her voice flat. "I was so mad, I didn't care."

Kay's absence is the only indication I have that what Lainey has done is truly bad. I don't have any relative experience, other than my initial desire to inflict some sort of pain or humiliation on James. Now that he's getting married to Whore-Bitch, the desire has resurfaced to the point that I can empathize.

"Can you take it back? Say it wasn't true?"

"No." I can tell by how quickly she answers that she's already looked for an out and found nothing. "I can't afford to take it back."

Kay comes back onto the deck, holding a short glass, with two fingers of something brown. "You said Vivian instructed us to help ourselves." She says to me, slightly lifting the glass.

Without looking at Lainey Kay asks, "So you decided to strike first? Figured it would hurt less if you played dirty and beat him to the punch?"

Lainey nods, and a tear makes its way down her face. "It doesn't hurt less." She says. "It's worse. I've become what I was afraid he would be, shitty."

"Well," Kay says, "what did Dad used to say?" She looks at me, but isn't waiting for an answer. "No point in asking how you stepped in the shit you're standing in. It stinks, so let's just figure out how to get it off."

Lainey exhales in gratitude. "It won't come off. I can't undo this. If I try to come clean and tell him what I've done, he'll never forgive me. I've started this dirty fight and now I'm in it, whether I like it or not."

I try to think of a way out, but we all know she's right. Admitting that she started a smear campaign leaves her with nothing, less than she started with. I wonder if there's enough value in doing the right thing to make it worth losing everything.

"Where are your fucking balls?" I ask, surprising myself most. "I'm out on the biggest limb I've eve been on, trying to find the right thing for me. So what? So what if you lose a bunch of stuff? At least if you end up with nothing, you'll still have you."

"I can't. I just can't."

"Of course you can." Kay and I say in unison. Apparently Vivian has rubbed off on me more than I thought, enough that I've brought this one thing to Kay too.

"Think about it." Kay says, and I wonder if it's possible that Lainey could do this. As easy as it seems, it's a much bigger decision when you're the one who could end up without a roof over your head.

CHAPTER 13

Dear Oprah,

I was watching Dr. Oz yesterday. My God, could that man be any cuter? I hope he's helping you with your thyroid problem, and I'm glad that you have access to the best. I know that must be stressful and difficult to cope with, just as I know how defeated anyone feels when they gain weight back. I just wanted to tell you that although I understand that you want to be the size you're comfortable with, I think you look fabulous. Really.

Regards,

Cates

Ps. Do you still own a home in Georgia? I was just wondering.

I made breakfast the next morning, letting the smell of bacon and coffee permeate the house and wake them up as it has greeted me so many days when I've walked through the door here. We ate with very little conversation. I couldn't tell if Kay and Lainey were tired or if it was the quiet of decisions yet to be made.

Not long after they left, I watered the garden, enjoying the time with Buddy by my side. When I came back in I remembered the trunk, and figured I might as well go through it now. I procrastinate enough at my own house.

Perhaps cleaning this out for Vivian will be counterproductive to the time I spent removing clutter from my own closet, but I know I can't throw out the dress with the green chiffon. There are a few old wool coats, smelling lightly of cedar. They have big plastic brown buttons, probably the height of fashion when they were new. As much as I want to keep them, I have a coat and despite the pockets being worn through, someone else can use them to keep warm. Beneath the coats is a fabric bag, like the ones my beloved Kate Spade bags came in. In them are several pairs of dress shoes, short stiletto heels in metallic shades, all with very pointy toes. I squeeze my foot into one, unsure if it's a size too small or if they're just remarkably uncomfortable. There's another fabric bag with small spools of lace, once white now dingy beige, a variety of buttons, and packets of clear plastic line, like you would see on fishing lures. I pull out the plastic line, thin as dental floss and wrap it around my pointer finger. It bends easily, but as soon as you let go of it, it returns to its original shape. I mindlessly string the buttons on it, wondering if Vivian used this to string popcorn as a Christmas tree decoration.

Then it hits me. This plastic line is what I should use to bead my jewelry. It's so perfect I can't believe I didn't realize this the second I pulled it from the bag. I have to go and grab my book and beads from the car. I only packed them to humor myself, as if I truly intended to work on it while I was here. I had figured that most likely I would buckle down and finish them at the last minute, the way I had with almost every homework assignment I'd ever been given.

Buddy must feel my excitement, racing me to the car for the beads, then back inside. I rub his head in a circular motion as if he is the magic genie of beading. Within minutes I know this is going to work. After the hours I spent with the metal wire, I have the motions down pat. Without the metal tips constantly pricking my fingers, I can move quickly, tying and threading over and over again.

By the end of the day I have ten necklaces ready to go. I only need thirty, and I have five days. If I keep the same pace, and I know I can go faster, I will have all thirty hats done with two days to spare for finishing touches. I thank God for working in this mysterious way. I don't have to feel guilty for procrastinating. I was meant to find this clear plastic thread, and it couldn't have happened any other way, any sooner or later. This must be how God works when you're exactly where you're supposed to be.

Preparation meets opportunity and it all falls into place. I fight temptation to celebrate, and push forward. By the time Vivian gets back, I have my thirty necklaces, and so much more. I have wraps of blue chiffon, layered around the hats. It's bigger than I ever imagined, this idea of mine. There are scarves, delicately wrapped around the base of the hat, accentuating the beads.

I imagine myself talking to Oprah, explaining how I came up with the idea, when my hats are on an OWN Favorite Things Christmas Spectacular. I can hear her saying how much she loves the concept, how she gave them to everyone on her staff. I'm sitting in one of her perfect chairs. I can picture Vivian beaming in the audience as I tell how her chiffon dress inspired the idea.

If Kay knew, she would be yelling at me, "You did WHAT?" Not Oprah, Oprah knows The Secret. I can see her in all her wisdom, nodding as I explain how I had to take the chance, that I spent all but what would cover the next month's bills when I bought the rolls of chiffon.

When I meet with Lainey's friend Rita, at her boutique, she is pleased. "Interesting…" she says, as I show her how the scarf can be pressed flat and worn around the hat under the jewelry with the clips I've sewn into the sides. This isn't the level of excitement I had hoped for, but she likes the idea. I have over-delivered, which is a huge step up from the embarrassment of the blue cheese. When I leave there is a check in my hand, half upfront, the other half when the hats sell.

It doesn't matter that half doesn't quite cover the cost of the materials. It's a start. This is no small victory, but the long awaited pay off from my beginning, my AHA moment! More than a little relieved that my days of financial decline are soon going to be behind me, I pick up champagne and invite Kay over to celebrate.

"Oh, Veuve Clicquot!" She says as soon as she sees the bottle. The first bottle goes quickly as I tell her that all thirty hats are at the boutique. Before she can ask, I tell her what she wants to know. She can't help that she is the oldest, always true to birth order traits, wanting specifics and monetary breakdowns.

"I'll turn a profit when sixty hats are sold." This must be satisfactory since there is no lecture about how much I spent on two bottles of champagne. I already feel worn out from my own excitement, like a kid who doesn't sleep the night before Christmas. "How's Lainey?" I ask.

Kay rolls her eyes. "You know what pisses me off?"

"People who don't use their blinkers." I answer, proof that I was listening when she called while sitting in traffic on her way over.

"That after I listened for hours on end as Lainey went on and on about how she wanted a peaceful divorce, that she's the one who made it ugly. She did this. And now that she's jacked it all up, she wants me to help her figure out how to fix it."

I uncork the other bottle and listen instead of telling her what we already know, that people do stupid shit when they're scared. "Sometimes it feels like she's changed, like I don't know her anymore."

"You do." I answer, but the words feel hollow.

"I don't know. Do you remember that song we used to sing in Brownies, the one that goes 'make new friends, but keep the old, one is silver and the other's gold'?"

I nod, humming the tune.

"They shouldn't teach kids that shit. They should tell little girls the truth. Some of your friends will change. Sometimes you grow up and grow apart, and some become assholes."

Her point isn't lost on me. I remember vividly the day I figured out that Jennifer Pierce and I would not in fact be best friends forever. She had a slumber party, and I overheard her telling Michelle Baker that she wished they were going to camp together instead of her going with me. It was crushing. I spent the following weeks in private mourning, too embarrassed to even tell my mom why I didn't want to go to camp anymore.

"What she did was bad," I say, making sure Kay knows that I get it, "but she didn't do it to you."

"That's not the point. The point is that the Lainey I know, or used to know, wouldn't have done that to anyone. She wouldn't have made up a lie, much less a big fat public lie, to get what she thinks she should have."

"I'm not defending her, but it's not like she's proud of what she did."

"Yeah, well, she's not exactly in a hurry to make it right either."

I laugh a little, even though it's not funny. "Making it right is going to suck. If she tells Michael what she did, I'm sure he'd be more than happy to let his divorce attorney eat her alive."

"And he'd have every right to. I don't know what happened in their marriage. That's between them and whomever they decide to share that with. What I do know is what didn't happen, he didn't cheat on her. If her lie ends up in some gossip blurb of the AJC, it's there forever in online archives."

"Wait, it's not in print yet?" I grab my laptop and bring it on the balcony for a quick search. There is nothing.

This doesn't seem to make Kay feel any better. "If it's not there, it's not because she didn't try. It means she didn't know the right people to tell."

"Yeah, but when we succeed with luck, we let that count. Can't it be enough that she failed with a little luck? She didn't do what she set out to do, and this time that was a good thing."

Kay sips her champagne, mulling this over. "If you talk to her, don't tell her it's not in the paper. Please."

I nod in agreement. "How was your date?" She hadn't mentioned it since our spa night, so I figured it didn't go well, but a change of subject seems in order.

Kay smiles. "It went well, but I don't want to talk about it. I know you can't jinx it by talking about it, but just in case."

The next morning, even though I wake up before my alarm goes off, Kay is already gone. This is part of the problem of living in a city without public transportation, if you're out drinking; you have to spend the night. We have MARTA, which is sort of a joke since the city is so spread out and the trains have a very limited coverage area. You could call a cab to go home, but you'd still have to deal with the hassle of getting your car in the morning.

I have two hours before I have to leave for Vivian's, so I stay in bed. I don't want to get up and make the coffee I have not acclimated to. I miss the smell of the good coffee, the breakfast blend and the chocolate cherry and crème brulee, flavors I used to switch between. It won't be long, I tell myself. Soon I will have the fancy coffee again.

My mind wanders to all the things I want but can't afford. All the twenty bucks here, thirty there, items that I can't justify now since I need that thirty, which wouldn't be enough for an oil change if I didn't have a coupon. Not to mention the slow drip coming from my kitchen sink that I can't afford to repair. Hair cut, brow wax, hair volumizing spray, the list could go on and on. And I miss my candles, the really good soy ones that permeate the room and burn for a long time. While these things could hardly be considered trappings of aristocracy, I miss them like the luxuries I now know they are.

After starting as an advertising assistant at twenty-two, making eighteen thousand dollars a year, I want the things I worked so hard to have. I make a list and put it on my board, the board that has pictures of the things I want in life. I never imagined that I would need to put the little things on there. As soon as I turn a profit, I will have them again.

When I get to Vivian's I'm glad that I didn't bother with coffee at home. She has a pot on, and it smells incredible, rich like dark chocolate. "Just in time," she greets me. "I was going to sit down for coffee and a cigarette." Only she can say this without the cigarette sounding trashy. She never smells like smoke, and her voice is clear, without the raspy sound of a smoker.

When I tell her this she says, "When I started smoking everything was different. There was an ad where an Olympic speed skater takes a break for a refreshing smoke. You saw cigarettes everywhere, not the dirty secret they are now. Lucille Ball smoked on her show, Dick Van Dyke did too. It was long before he was President, but even Ronald Reagan was in ads for Chesterfield's. For my generation there was nothing rebellious about it. We thought it had benefits other than being glamorous, which at the time it was. Besides, you and I don't smoke the same things." She goes inside and returns, handing me a pack of her cigarettes. I have never noticed them before. When she gets out more than one, they are usually in a silver case that matches her lighter.

"Additive free, 100% natural tobacco." I read aloud.

"They add a bunch of chemicals to those," she says, gesturing to my pack. "Indians have been smoking tobacco forever, without sounding like they're going to cough up a lung. It's the stuff they add that makes them burn fast, release more smoke, and makes them a lot worse for you."

"Really? I didn't know that."

Vivian shrugs. "Well it may not be a fact, but I'm eighty years old and have earned my right to theorize."

Vivian shows me the seeds we have planted in what she calls "the incubator", a plastic container, with pods of dirt and a clear lid. I can't believe that what was just a mound of dirt last week is a thin green stalk, no thicker than a blade of grass, but tall enough to reach the lid. "Your herbs!" She says to me, as if I did something more than the task she gave me.

With guidance from Vivian, I take the small delicate pods and plant some in pots, others in the ground. Under Buddy's watchful eye, I complete Mojito Lane and wonder if Buddy thinks of himself as the audience or the foreman. It's only as I'm driving back home that I realize I forgot to tell Vivian my good news, that I finished the hats.

Being diligent I set to work on the next thirty hats. Inspired by the ambience at Vivian's, I listen to Ella Fitzgerald as I string more beads. I imagine that before too long, I will have an employee, someone with fingers more nimble than mine to do this. At the rate I'm going I will have the next thirty hats ready to replace the first thirty as soon as they're sold. I get out my calendar, carefully marking when the next bills are due. I know I can make it.

Christian calls to tell me that he stopped by the boutique and saw my hats on display in the window. "We should celebrate." He says. I hesitate, knowing that as close as I am to being on my feet again, I can't afford it yet. "My treat," He says, "Let me take you out. I'll pick you up." It's too tempting. Before I know it, I'm showered and getting dressed.

"Maggiano's okay?" He asks as I get into his car. Christian looks remarkably handsome, wearing a black button down shirt. Even though he is seated, I can tell that he's wearing nice designer jeans.

"I love Maggiano's!" I really do. If I hadn't spent the last five years counting carbs, I would go there on a regular basis. We get a high top table in the bar area. Christian orders a bottle of wine, so much better than the Two Buck Chuck I've been drinking at home. We decide to split mussels as an appetizer. They come to the table in a bowl of creamy garlic broth. Between the piano music and the candle on the table, this feels cozy, like the best date I've been on in a long time. If Christian didn't have a boyfriend, it would be incredibly romantic. Just as the girl singing by the piano begins her rendition of "All or Nothing at All", I spot James at the bar. I can tell he's waiting for a table because he has one of those electric buzzers that goes off when your table is ready.

"Oh shit!" I say, locking eyes with Christian. "Don't look." Unlike most people, this doesn't cause him to instantly pan the area searching to find what he's not supposed to look at.

"What is it?" He asks, not taking his eyes off me.

"It's him." I answer. "James, the cheater." Even though this is how I think of James now, my heart is racing. Other than when I planned to meet him out, I haven't run into him once since we broke up. I had even wondered before, since it seemed odd that it had never happened, if we'd been at the same place before and he left as soon as he saw me.

"Shit. I don't know what to do." My face feels hot, and I hope it isn't turning red.

"Don't do anything." Christian says, a thought that hadn't occurred to me.

"What if he sees me?" I sit motionless, like a deer in the woods, like he won't spot me if I'm perfectly still. I wish I hadn't spent money to get my hair blown out the last time I saw him. If I hadn't, I might have enough money to go to the salon and cover the ten bright white hairs sprouting from my crown. God, I hope I brushed mascara over them today, I think, bringing my hand to my head in hopes that I will feel the slight roughness the mascara leaves.

"What if he sees you? If he comes over, say 'hi'. Cate, it's perfect. You're having dinner with me, your boyfriend, remember?" As soon as it registers, I want him to see me. I want him to see me so badly I can't think of enough ways to draw attention to myself. If there was a sexy way to start choking, and have Christian perform the Heimlich, I would do it.

"Hey," Christian says, putting his hand over mine, drawing me back from the inner workings of a mad woman. "Relax, or I'll start singing show tunes." Miraculously, I do. As I look at his face, smiling at me, I'm back in the moment with him.

"You should be a hypnotist." I tell him, and it's only then that I notice that James has walked over to our table.

"I didn't mean to interrupt," James says, "I just wanted to say hi." Christian moves his hand from the top of mine and extends it to James.

"I'm Christian." He says casually. James shakes his hand without saying a word. "And you are?" Christian asks.

"James." He says, before clearing his throat.

"How are you?" I ask, as if he's a normal person, someone I genuinely hope is well. I hear it in my voice and wonder if it's possible that I no longer have hard feelings.

"I'm good." James says. He pauses briefly before saying again, "I didn't mean to interrupt."

"Would you like to join us?" Christian asks, as if there's room to pull up another chair.

"Oh, no." James answers. "Thank you, but my table should be ready soon. Anyway, it was nice to meet you, Christian. Cate." He nods at me before walking to the hostess stand.

I smile at Christian, who's pouring more wine for both of us. "You like that?" He asks me, eyebrows raised and smiling. I know it's petty, just like I know that Christian is gay and not my boyfriend, but I do like it. More than anything I like that the bitterness that has been stewing inside me for all of these months is finally dissipating.

CHAPTER 14

Dear Oprah,

I just want to say thank you. I'm sure you got some ugly emails after the Mike Tyson interview, but this is not one of them. You handled that with such grace. I enjoyed it the first time I saw it and today when it aired again. His story had such resonance with me, and I think you felt it too. I couldn't hold back the tears when he said, "I'm tired of losing. I wanna win now." I never would have thought that Mike Tyson could articulate the way I feel in my life. And I'm grateful to you for that. Maybe someday I can be as honest about my shortcomings and fears as he was.

Regards,

Cate

P.S. Any thought of bringing your show back? I'm living off reruns and starting to feel like I'm running on fumes.

In the two weeks that my hats have been in the boutique, five have sold. Rita, the boutique owner says that's really good, but I have no way of knowing if she's right. After all of my years of analyzing sales and marketing techniques, my own hats are in a store that I know nothing about.

I don't know the boutique's sales volume, the frequency the shoppers visit the store, or how much they spend on an average visit. All of the factors that I would calculate to let someone else know whether or not their venture is successful, I don't have for my own business. I remind myself that there is an inevitable learning curve and head to Vivian's, eager to clear my head in the garden.

Oprah says that every home has its own feeling. This is true. Despite the fact that when I get to Vivian's there is no inviting scent coming from the stove top or even the coffee pot, it still feels like the most welcoming place I know. I wonder if this is how my parent's house would feel to me if they still lived in the home I grew up in. I call out to Vivian to let her know that I'm there, but there's no response, no sound of Buddy coming to greet me.

I step out onto the back deck. Vivian is at the table, smoking, in a long floral night gown, all but disappearing under the fabric. Buddy is lying on top of her feet, not beside them. There's no sign that she's heard me, so I back up to knock on the door, hoping I won't startle her. Buddy turns his head to look at me, but doesn't move. "Vivian…" I say quietly.

"Come on out, Cate." She still doesn't look at me. Her eyes are fixed on the garden, but I don't have to see her face. I recognize the handkerchief she's gripping with her hand that isn't holding a cigarette. As much as

I feel like I'm intruding, I can't stop myself from awkwardly hugging her neck. For the first time, Vivian seems small to me.

"Do you want me to leave?" I ask, unaware that I'm holding my breath for a response, praying that she doesn't say yes.

"No, honey. Make some coffee, will you?"

"Of course I can." I answer.

When I returned with the coffee I set hers down in front of her, but wasn't sure if I should sit down. As if reading my mind Vivian said, "Why don't you sit down and smoke with me? Grieving alone is like drinking alone, you should only do it when it's the only option."

I didn't know what to say, so I said nothing. I lit a cigarette, and sat with her in silence.

Her pain was so palpable it was overwhelming. I've only felt that way a couple of times, both as a child. When Kay had broken her arm or the time she needed stitches, it hurt like it was my own exposed, flesh and bone unnaturally feeling the air.

After a while Vivian sipped her coffee. "Thank you." She said. "I just didn't want to make the coffee this morning," her voice started to break but she cleared her throat and continued, "Didn't want another reminder that life goes on." Vivian looked at me, and I could see her eyes, puffy and rimmed red with sadness. "I'm glad you're here. I really am." She lit another cigarette.

"Do you want more coffee?" I asked. "A warm up?" There was some left in both of our cups, but the morning air had already started to cool it.

Vivian smiled and said, "Yes, and grab the Bailey's from the liquor cabinet too."

As she poured the Bailey's into her coffee she said, "Normally I only do this at Christmas or on my birthday. Honey, I don't mean to be a stick in the mud, but I lost a friend last night, and well, I won't pretend it doesn't hurt like hell because it does."

"Oh, Vivian!" I said, "I'm so sorry." My eyes welled up with tears, and I leaned over to hug her again.

Tears began to stream down her face, faster than the handkerchief could reach them. "Thank you, Cate. I can't tell you how much it means to me that you feel like it's sad too."

"Of course I do."

"Oh honey, you're too young to even know how sweet that is." Her hanky must have been wet since she was now wiping her face on the sleeve of her nightgown. I went and grabbed the box of Kleenex from her bathroom and brought it to her. "When you get to be older, you think the worst thing that happens is when your husband dies. And by God, when I lost my husband, I thought that was the worst. Then as you get older, more and more people you know die, and I guess you get used to that. It's a reminder that you're old, that you're going to die, and I suppose it's natural to get used to that too, and I have." She nods, like it's important for me to know that this is true. "Then your friends die. What no one tells you is the worst thing; that eventually as more and more of your friends die, no one else seems to think it should be as sad for you anymore." Her bottom lip quivered and tears streamed down her face. I pulled my chair closer, careful not to bump into Buddy.

"Vivian, I don't know what to say." There's a lump in my throat so big that I feel like I'm trying to swallow her pain.

She blows her nose and wipes her face as if she's certain there aren't more tears on the way, and looks me straight in the eyes. "You don't have to say anything. It means so much to have you here."

I wonder if it wasn't one of my gardening days, if Vivian would be sitting here alone and realize that she is just like the rest of us. Vivian is single, and when you're single your friends are the people who are there when you shouldn't be alone. They're the ones who mark the events in our lives, our self created families who show up when it matters.

"And more importantly, I never thought that at this point in my life, I would make a new friend. Here you are, my friend." I felt myself smiling, proud to be Vivian's friend. She put her hand over mine and added, "You're a fine person, Cate. I know you're having a hard time. The world seems awful big when you're looking for answers, but I know everything is going to work out just fine for you because you're asking the right questions." Even though she had lost a friend, Vivian was still making me feel better. I tried not to cry, and for the first time in a long time, it wasn't out of self pity. It was because I could see how lucky I was.

CHAPTER 15

Dear Oprah,

I was watching another rerun and Paula Deen (probably not your favorite person right about now) was on your show saying there's no sin in failure, the sin is in not trying. As much as that spoke to me, I'm ashamed to admit that I can't get out of my pajamas today. I feel like a failure. I know better than to put stock in that emotion, but I can't shake the feeling that I'm a fraud. What if this is who I really am, someone who just wants to wallow in a Fudge Round?

Cate

Despite all of my attempts to envision the life I'm trying to create, sometimes you have to see things as they are, not as how you want them to be. I don't know why I thought that everything would fall into place when I sorted out what to do with my life, but that's what I believed. I don't have a great sense of relief, but maybe that will come with sustainable income, when I'm not worrying about the bills. I try to tell myself that

I have to believe in the work that I have done. I can't give in to self doubt. This is all happening for a reason.

I try to remind myself what Vivian told me the other day. She said, "Things take time. A lot of people won't wait, don't know how to wait. They're looking for instant gratification." I responded that she must think my generation is ridiculously impatient with cell phones and instant messaging, and me in my quest for overnight success.

Vivian shook her head and laughed. She said, "No, honey, that's been happening forever. You think there wasn't a day when my generation was hearing about how fast we had everything? Every generation has opinions about the ones following it, and they all sound the same."

I can't escape my own thoughts, the inevitable uncertainties running through my head. The doorbell rings, and I'm glad that Jill is here for dinner. I know she would rather go out and have a waitress instead of being here, where I'm constantly getting up and down to check on the chicken in the oven or refreshing our beverages. I too would prefer not to have our conversation interrupted every five minutes, but like most things in life, it is what it is.

I open the door to see Jill, who's hair is back to light brown with subtle golden highlights. It has only been a few weeks since she dyed it the rich shade I would call Rebound Chocolate. "Hey, you switched back!" I said, somewhat surprised that the salon was able to return her exact coloring, as if it had never been altered.

"Yeah," she said, handing me a case of Stella Artois, her favorite beer. "It took all day. They had to do it in stages, to make sure they didn't strip too much, then by the time they were done with that, adding back in the highlights...seriously, I was there for nine hours."

"How much did that cost?" There was no reason to sound accusatory, but we both heard the tone, the judgment in my asking. Six months ago I would have spent the same amount of money at a salon without batting an eyelash, but now I'd changed into someone who was sickened by the amount of groceries that would buy. I guess this is why people usually choose friends that have similar income to theirs. This is awkward, and Jill shouldn't have to apologize for her position.

"Sorry," I said quickly. "It's obviously not your fault that I don't have money for salon visits now. I've turned into a thirty-two year old woman who constantly has her hair in a pony tail. And look!" I tilted my head down, showing her the white strands at my part.

"Cate, if you need to get your hair done, I'll give you the money."

"Thank you, but no. I can't let you do that."

"Why not? Remember, Bank of Jill, Bank of Cate? If I have it and you need it, it's yours. Like years ago when my car died and you lent me money for a down payment?"

"Because this isn't like that. First of all, you had to have a car. I can go without salon visits. I'm a grown ass woman. I've made a choice. I wanted to branch out on my own, find my purpose in life, and I have to take it as it comes."

"So, you can't have some help?"

"Listen, I have done everything that I can do, and now I have to wait. I spent the last three days going to different boutiques and got two more stores to carry my hats. Until those sell, I can't afford anything. When they do sell, I need to buy more materials. I have to wade my way through this."

"That doesn't mean that you have to struggle." I could tell by the way she was looking at me that she thought I was being stubborn.

"It does. Neither one of us are trust-fund babies. You're where I was six months ago. You work hard to afford the things you want. What if you lost your job? You need to keep your money for your own rainy day, and for your own enjoyment. I really appreciate the offer though."

Jill sighed. "Let me know if you change your mind. I mean it."

I grabbed two Stella's from the fridge, and we headed out to my balcony. After I took a few sips of beer, I told Jill what I had decided. "I won't change my mind. I'm trading in my car tomorrow."

"What? You love that car! And it's just starting to be warm, convertible weather!"

"Yeah, I do. But it's just a car. I worked my ass off to trade in my beaten up Honda Civic before, and I can do it again."

"Trade it in for what?"

I smiled. "Another used Honda Civic. Don't worry; I'm sure my old one is in a junk yard by now." When I had finally traded in my Civic for the BMW, it had over two hundred thousand miles on it and rust on the hood and bumper. The yellow foam cushion on both the driver's and passenger's seats was pushing through the ripped worn fabric. Kay told me I should be thankful that they gave my three hundred dollars for it, instead of charging me to remove it from the lot.

"Is money that tight?"

"Yes." I confessed to spending the rest of my savings on materials. Unlike Kay, Jill understood that sometimes you have to spend money to make money. I had spent the money, so now it was time to trade in my car and cut the monthly payment in half.

Jill rubbed her chin with her forefinger. "It sounds like you've thought this through. Good for you."

I did feel good about it. On some level that car had been a status symbol for me. Not because it was a BMW, but because it was the convertible that I had always wanted. It was two years old when I bought it, but to me it represented the kind of life I had achieved. That car went with the life I had, working for the wrong things. Just like the consumers that I used to manipulate into buying an ideal with my marketing strategies, I had bought into something too. As much as I hoped that I would have the financial stability to get back to where I was, I now wanted it on different terms.

The next morning I got up and went to the Honda dealership. I would buy a used Civic, whatever it took to cut my payment in half. When I pulled into the lot I noticed the man standing on the lot with a notepad, jotting something down from a window sticker. He was wearing Khakis and a button-down shirt with brown loafers. He looked like an old frat boy, with thinning blonde hair. He noticed me too and flashed a big grin. *Not this time,* I thought to myself, knowing I was not susceptible to the lure of new car smell or upgrades.

I parked and walked over to the used cars that were off to the side. I needed a car with low miles. I owed a little over nineteen thousand on my BMW, so I looked for cars that were in the eight to ten thousand dollar range. A lot of them were manual transmissions. It had been a while, but I knew how to drive one.

My dad had insisted that Kay and I learn on one, his old Isuzu Trooper. "Almost half the cars out there are stick shift," he had said, and that was true at the time. "If you can only get into every other car and drive, you can't drive." Never afraid to scare us for the sake of a lesson, he had continued, "Say you get abducted, and you get a chance to escape and the only car is a stick shift. My girls are going to know how to drive one." And so we did.

"Perfect car for a teenager." The frat man was standing beside me.

"What?" I asked.

"My son is turning sixteen in a few months. I've been looking at getting him one of these myself."

"Oh God," I said, wondering if I did need money from Jill to go to the salon. How the hell did I look old enough to have a teenager? "No, this is for me." I saw him look back to where I had barked my beamer. "I'm cutting back on expenses."

"Oh, well that's ok." He rocked back on the heels of his loafers.

"Good, I'm glad that's ok." I said. I was quickly losing the good, responsible feeling I had when I pulled on the lot. I wanted to yell, I'm so glad you approve, that is such a load off!

He had already started into his spiel, oblivious that I wanted to slap him. His head moved like a bobble head doll's above his collar, "You gotch'ur sun roof, you gotch'ur illuminated entry, you gotch'ur power windows, with driver one touch down feature…" I'd already looked at them online, and this car was right in line with the Blue Book value.

I interrupted him, "Is this the drive out price?" I asked, pointing at the sticker, "No hidden add-ons?"

"Well, yes, but we can get this closer to what your used to, add a six disc CD changer to it. Just because you're moving down from a BMW, it doesn't mean that we can't add some nice features to make it a little less painful."

I was starting to wish I had a different salesperson until I spotted the alternative. There was a short squatty man helping a woman about my age not far from us. His belly was big and round, and seemed to have swallowed his belt below it. I heard him call her "little lady" and figured this was as good as it would get.

"No extra features." I said, "Let's get started on the paperwork." We went inside and sat down at his desk, big and metal, like my school teachers' had. I handed him the paperwork on my BMW. In exchange he offered me a bottle of water or coffee that looked like it had been sitting for a while. I took the bottle of water and waited while he went into the back to start the paperwork. After fifteen minutes had passed with no sign of him, I was wishing that I had told him I was going outside to smoke. Just as I was about to leave a note on his desk, he returned.

"How much are you going to put down?" He asked.

"Um, I wasn't going to put anything down, just a simple trade." I answered.

He sat down in the chair beside me. "You see, the problem is that you're upside down on the BMW." I stared at him, thinking that couldn't be true. It was slightly below the Blue Book value when I bought it. I had been paying on it for two years.

"That means you owe more than it's worth. We've seen this a lot lately, the value of luxury cars has gone down as a result of the economy."

"That can't be." I said, confident that I would go to another dealership and trade it in, although the knot in my chest was starting to tell me differently.

"I printed out the Blue Book value on the BMW, you can see for yourself." He handed me a piece of paper. His tone softened and he spoke slowly. "You need over four thousand dollars to make up the difference between what it's worth and how much you owe. We can't roll the negative equity over into the Civic, because the bank won't lend you that amount for that car."

"Shit." I said, my hand instinctively moved to cover my mouth. "I don't have four thousand dollars. I don't have a thousand dollars. If I did I wouldn't be here."

"Here's my card." He said, handing it to me. "If something changes, give me a call."

I walked to my car, trying not to panic. This was something I was going to do, not something I had to do. An option was eliminated, no reason to cry, although that was exactly what I was starting to do.

I drove to Vivian's as planned. My car that I had loved and been so happy with, suddenly felt like the weight of the world on my shoulders. I had thought I was going to be sad to drive off the lot, leaving it there. Instead I'm leaving with the sick feeling that I'm stuck with it.

By the time I get to Vivian's I have composed myself. I walk in the door, Buddy running to greet me. I don't know if it's the music, the upbeat tempo of Louis Armstrong or the smell of roasting chicken, but the energy is palpable, cheery. I wish I lived here.

Vivian walks into the kitchen from out back, "Cate, you're here!" She says, as if she's surprised to see me, but I'm right on time.

"Have I got something for you! You're going to love it. Follow me." She walks back outside. There are rows of the small containers she uses for planting seeds, all filled with small green plants, each a few inches tall. The sun feels good, warm on my face.

"More herbs?"

"Better! They're moonvines and morning glories. But the moonvines, that's what you're going to love. They're the ones I showed you in the greenhouse."

She holds them up, looking at them closely. I look too, but I'm not sure what I'm looking at. "See, these are strong. They're going to do great in the ground." She walks over to the side of the deck, where the wood railing begins. "These are both vines, so you want to plant them in the ground where they have something to climb. We'll plant the morning glories around the trellis at the garden entrance, but you're in charge of the moonvines. They should go here, by the deck. You want them close."

"Close?"

"Oh honey, you're going to enjoy these. They're the best thing about summer. You want them here around the deck. You plant them in the ground, on the other side of the railing. You're going to need to watch them, guide them as they make their way up the wooden rungs. When they start getting tall, you're going to need to make sure they don't get tangled."

I started rolling up my sleeves so I could get to work. Vivian put up her hand to stop me. "You know how you're always telling me that I should write a book about gardening?" She asked.

I nodded. It's amazing how much knowledge she has in her head, all these tiny tricks that she's learned that seem to make all the difference. If nothing else, I wish she'd write them down for my benefit. "If I were going to, it would have only one chapter: moonvines. They're special."

I wondered if they were finicky like orchids, if I was going to ruin them in less than a week. "Are you sure you want me in charge of them? What if I mess them up?"

"You won't mess them up. You, my dear, have a green thumb."

"Whatever that is, I don't have it. I have killed every plant I've brought into my home, even the snake grass. Christian said it's also called Mother-in-Law's tongue because no matter what you do to it, you can't stop it. So I bought one, and apparently you can stop it."

"Doesn't count." Vivian said, shaking her head. "You're talking about indoor plants, which are totally different. You don't have a lot of light in your place, so move the snake grass to the place that gets some sun and see what happens. But that's not what a green thumb is about. A green thumb is about sensing what the plants need. Two people can go to a nursery and buy tomato plants, and one person's may get big and tall and produce big juicy tomatoes and the others may hardly flower at all. People will say it's about the soil, sun and rain, which is part of it, but it's not the whole thing. Those plants don't live by set directions, like give me this much water at this time, every other day. They're living things, and can be affected by random elements in different ways. When you have a green thumb, you have a perception of what those needs are and you adapt to the plant. Look what you did over there." She motioned to where the herbs are growing in with the dahlias and the irises. I've been in charge of watering them since we planted the bulbs.

"I didn't do anything. I followed your instructions and watered them. I held the hose."

"You did a lot more then holding the hose. You adjusted the nozzle to the right amount of pressure, as you sensed it, for those plants. Then you watered it for a certain amount of time. You sensed how much water they needed." Her gardening gloves were dirty, so she wiped the sweat off her brow with her arm. "That's instinct, plain and simple. And when you have an instinct about plants, it's called a green thumb."

Trying to feel for myself, the confidence that Vivian had in me, I set out planting the moonvines. I planted each one a hand's width apart, leaving space for their roots to grow. Vivian likes to wear gloves, but I don't. It feels good to me, the dirt on my fingers, connected to the earth. I find myself praying, that in time the beading will come naturally to me, that it will fall into a rhythm like this where I can lose myself in it. The burden of my car begins to lift. Then I pray for Lainey, that her weight will be lifted too. That she won't feel burdened by things either, that she will find peace and be brave enough to do the right thing. Each vine went into the ground, with hope and a prayer.

CHAPTER 16

Dear Oprah,

I wish people would leave you alone about marrying Stedman. It's hard enough to be a single woman, with people always asking you about your personal life, as if it's their right to know. It must be that much harder for you. I'm sure Maya Angelou probably gave you some wonderful words of wisdom, and it doesn't even bother you now. But if it does still get under your skin, I really do understand.

Regards,

Cate

Ps. If you do want to marry Stedman, I hope he knows how lucky he is.

I finally get the call. The first boutique has sold all of my hats. She has a check, for me! When I go to pick up the money, she asks when I can get her more inventory. She has asked for fifty this time. I tell her I will have to get back to her later in the day with a time frame. I don't want to look at the check in front of her, and I don't know if it's enough for me to buy materials. Apparently one woman loved them so much, she bought ten of them, to give them as gifts. I'm so excited that I call Kay from the parking lot.

By the time Kay meets me at the wine bar, I have already finished a glass. The weather is perfect Atlanta spring, and I wish I had one hat left so that I could wear it now. At least then I could cover up my hair.

"Oh my God, Cate, I'm so proud of you! This is huge!" She hugs me.

"You have no idea!" Now that the fear of failing miserably has passed, I can finally tell her that I spent my savings on supplies.

"You did what?" I could tell by the look on her face, the older sister thinks-you're-so-stupid look, that she didn't approve.

"See why I didn't tell you before? But look, it turned out fine. If I hadn't invested the money, I wouldn't have had the hats to sell. I tried to get a loan from the credit union, but they wouldn't give me one. It was my only choice."

"Ok," she said, her tone clearly reluctant to admit that I was right. "What if they hadn't sold?"

I shrugged, "I don't know. I would have figured something out. I left myself a month's worth of living expenses in the bank."

"That's good." Kay said, but the look on her face made it clear that she wanted to lecture me.

"But it did work. That's the point, that's why we're here celebrating! Anyway, what's new with you? I stopped by your place twice last week and you weren't home, on school nights."

"I've been seeing that guy." Kay answered.

"Does he have a name yet, or are you still afraid to jinx it?"

"His name is Adam. He's nice, he's funny. He's cute, but there's no spark. And I keep going out with him, like if I give it a chance maybe we'll develop some chemistry. There's nothing wrong with him, but I'm tired of feeling like as long as he doesn't have some major flaw, I have to give it a chance."

"Why would you have to give it a chance? If you're not feeling it, quit seeing him."

"Because Cate, I'm thirty-five and single."

"I'm thirty-two and single."

"That's different. You were recently engaged, you're not far removed from possibility. I haven't had a serious relationship in years."

"Removed from possibility? Geez, Kay, I don't know where you got this shit, but you need to return it."

Kay shook her head. "You don't know what it's like, dating in your thirties. You were with James for two years, and you haven't been dating since you broke up. It's different, and it's only gotten worse since I turned thirty-five."

"Kay, if this is about the men with kids thing, you're probably meeting more men with kids because you're an elementary school teacher. You just need to go out more."

"It's not that. It's other people, like I have to come up with an explanation why I'm thirty-five and single, never married." Kay fanned her face with her hands. I know this move. She always does this when she's trying not to cry, and it rarely works. "Oh shit." She dabbed around the inner corners of her eyes with a beverage napkin. "I don't know why I'm so emotional, could be PMS."

To an onlooker I would seem cold, seated across from her and giving no reaction when she is obviously upset. But if I did anything, worst of all would be if I moved to hug her right now, she would start bawling. Kay would not want to bawl in the wine bar, so I sat and waited.

When her eyes were successfully dried, she resumed. "It's like I have to explain what's wrong with me, why nobody wants me." She immediately began fanning her face again.

"Who thinks nobody wants you? What the fuck? You could have married the wrong person if you wanted to. You could have a boyfriend right now. That guy Dennis from the coffee shop asks me about you every time I see him. How have you turned the fact that you don't want to settle, that you want the whole she-bang, the right guy for you, into nobody wanting you?"

Kay looked like I'd asked her to solve a calculus problem in her head. "I don't know."

"That's like if I said I feel like I have to explain why I'm single, why I wasn't enough for James, why he cheated on me. Different, but equally ridiculous. Kay, I'm not just saying this because you're my sister, I'm proud of you. At any time you could have decided that you were lonely and wanted to be with some Mr. Almost Right, and you haven't. You're waiting until the real thing comes along, and I think that's fucking admirable."

"Thank you." She sniffed. "I wish other people saw it that way."

"Who?" She didn't answer, confirming what I thought, some bitchy teacher at her school had said something that made her feel like shit. This had happened before, some unhappily married and bitter coworker, who was probably jealous of Kay, had made comments to Kay implying that she wasn't complete because she wasn't married.

"Kay, remember what you told me when Barbara used to make snide comments to me all the time? You said that the only person who defines me, is me. That I was too smart to let her opinions affect what I thought about myself."

Kay agreed with her own advice, commenting on how smart it was. I hoped she took it to heart. Her thinking that nobody wanted her was sickening to me. Later that night when I went to bed, it haunted my thoughts. How often, I wondered, do we let other people change how we see ourselves? Why is it that unless you're a narcissist, it's so much easier to believe the bad about yourself than the good?

CHAPTER 17

Dear Oprah,

I realize that if there was ever the slightest possibility that you would read one of my letters, this will be the email that causes your staff to block all future emails from me. All the same, I have to send it. I have to be honest with you.

When you announced that the next season would be your last of the Oprah Winfrey Show. I wanted to be happy for you. I knew that you must have your reasons. You're the wisest person I know. Ok, so you don't know me, but I feel like I really know you. And I was heartbroken. You were moving on, and I wasn't ready.

You have been a constant for most of my life, every weekday at four o'clock. As pathetic as it may sound, I don't know what I'm supposed to do without you. I always planned on going to a taping of the Oprah Show, and if I was lucky it was going to be when you had your Favorite Things show or something. Now that ship has sailed. And I haven't sorted out my life yet. I never really thought about your show ending, but I wouldn't have thought it would be when I need you most.

I'm sorry this is such a miserable email, but it's the truth. Because the truth is I'm still wishing that you would adopt me.

Regards,

Cate

There are no two ways about it; I'm going to have to buy more chiffon. I have enough beads and I ordered more hats, but the boutique owner said the chiffon had added a level of charm that made all the difference. She seemed much more excited than she was when I first showed them to her, and thought we should raise the price, which seems like a good idea to me too since I'm worrying about paying my bills. After spending all of the money I made on more chiffon, I was less than eager to hear that the other boutiques had sold out of them as well. I worked with all of the materials that I had, and was still short but trying to think of it as a good thing.

Jill got tickets to see Diana Krall at Chastain Amphitheatre. She said she wanted to go, and invited me along, but I know better. Jill doesn't own one Diana Krall CD, she bought them because she knew I wanted to go and couldn't afford the tickets.

It was warm spring weather, with a light breeze, so I decided to wear one of my hats. They weren't so big that they would block anyone's view, and I could be my own advertisement. I chose my favorite. The chiffon was light green, the shade I bought that looked like Vivian's dress, with angled beads that looked like jade mixed with opalescent round beads. They complimented each other perfectly, and really stood out in contrast against the black hat. I wore my dark Cookie Johnson skinny jeans that were featured on Oprah and a black dressy tank top, so the hat would stand out.

"My God," Jill said, when I got to her place. "You definitely have an eye for what works. I'm so proud of you!"

I let myself be proud of me too, and off we went to the concert. Diana Krall was amazing, perfectly clear voice, but with a depth that defies her age. The fact that she played the piano while she sang reminded me of the awe I feel when I watch a hockey game, because not only do they play something similar to a mixture of la crosse and rugby, they're doing it on ice skates. Here Diana was singing with a beautifully well trained voice, and tickling the ivories with incredible skill, like it was the most natural thing in the world. When she covered Joni Mitchell's Case of You, I could hardly wait until the end of the song to applaud. Even though Jill would rather be at a Brooks and Dunn concert, I could tell she was impressed too. I had such a good time I didn't wish for a minute that I was there on a date, even though we were surrounded by couples.

When we got up to leave I heard a clicking noise on the concrete beneath me, followed by a few more in rapid fire succession. "What was that?" I asked Jill, who was already bending over to see if we had dropped something.

"Hold still." She said, and more clicking sounds followed. "Oh, shit!" She said, as she stood up, holding out her hand. As I tilted my head to see what she was holding, there were little clicks everywhere. In her hand was a mixture of green and opalescent beads. I should have taken off my hat right then and there to prevent more from dropping, but it didn't occur to me until I was bent over, trying to collect them. Luckily Jill thought to remove it from my head and place it on the bench behind us, then proceeded to help me gather the beads, which were rolling around in front of us like a game of marbles.

By the time we got back to Jill's place I had calmed down considerably, which was a very good thing considering that at one point when we were collecting the beads from the floor, I thought I was going to have a panic attack. Actually I thought I was having a heart attack, but when Jill pointed out that heart attacks don't generally happen as a result of broken jewelry, I had to agree that it was anxiety induced.

At first I thought that maybe I didn't have the knots tied correctly at the end of the strand, but I quickly realized that the clasp would had to have broken as well. I felt much better when Jill brought it to my attention that this hat was the last one I made today, and I had probably rushed after deciding that I was making one to wear tonight. It wasn't that I wanted to believe her, it seemed the most logical explanation since I had tied every knot with pain staking detail and this was the first one I had made quickly. It was still unnerving, so I was glad that I had planned to spend the night at her place and could get liquored up.

I woke up with a hell of a hangover, but I had promised Vivian I would help with the garden today. Spring is her busiest time with the garden. We had to spray all of the newly planted vegetables to keep aphids away.

Aphids feed on plants by making a small puncture, and eating on the sap that is released. The plants need the sap to carry nutrients through it. Aphids are really small, but they can destroy a plant. In my mind they're the Barbara's and Alexis's of gardening. Because in addition to the fact that aphids are mostly females, even when it seems like they're not doing a lot of damage, their presence can eat you alive from the inside.

Lady bugs eat aphids, so it's a good sign to see them. They were in abundance at Vivian's, but you can't leave all the work to them. You see ants would be predators of aphids also, like the lady bugs. But when the aphids eat the sap out of the plant, they leave behind a sticky substance, which is the part of the sap they can't digest. The ants will eat that substance, and can actually get high off of it. Then the ants, to maintain their supply of the goods, will actually begin to protect the aphids.

It's a rather strange dynamic, but so is the dynamic between mean girls and their entourages. If there weren't a network of tasters, liking what they get out of the deal, it wouldn't continue so easily.

Vivian's already outside, spraying the plants when I get there. My hangover will have no reprieve, no coffee or time to sit before we get started. Luckily I took Tylenol before heading over, which should kick in soon. Buddy comes over to greet me, and I give Vivian a wave while petting his velvety soft head, trying to look cheery despite the pulsing behind my eyes.

We work side by side in silence, carefully spraying the plants a mist of protection against the aphids. Vivian's lips are moving, and I wonder if she is praying. The quiet is working wonders for my head, despite the pressure I feel when I bend over. We pull weeds as we spray, multitasking. I lose track of time, in my thoughts, wondering when Oprah knew that she was on the right track. I wonder if it's instinctive, or if you know all along. For some reason I can't relax and enjoy the progress I've made with the hats. It's not until all the plants have been treated, and Vivian asks if I want to take a lunch break with her, that I'm aware that hours have passed.

When we walk into the house Vivian asks, "Chicken salad, ok?" I nod enthusiastically, and she pulls a container out of the refrigerator. It's homemade chicken salad, with slivered almonds. She hands me a loaf of bread, and I assemble the sandwiches while she decides between her homemade jars of pickles. After she settles on dill, she brings the jar over, and puts one on each of our plates. "Should I put some music on?" She asks me.

"It's up to you." I say, and then I tell her about how at home I always eat with the TV on. I know it's a bad habit, but I hate eating alone in silence.

"I don't watch television anymore." Vivian says. I wonder if she's ever seen Oprah, and I have to ask. "Well I don't live in a cave…sure, I've seen Oprah on at Betty's or someone else's house. I used to turn on the TV every now and then, but then one time I was watching, and I thought, this is just trash."

Not that there's anything to debate, but I wonder what specific trash would be a deal breaker for her. Was it when they showed that guy's ass on NYPD Blue? That was a big deal at the time. I figure it was probably something like Melrose Place, but decide to ask anyway.

"No, it was a moisturizer commercial." She answers. "After you turn sixty your bladder thinks every good laugh, hard cough, or sneezing fit is a time to let loose. It's awful. One night I was watching a program, I don't even remember what it was, and this model, who couldn't have been a day older than thirty-five, comes on the screen talking about how to grow old gracefully. I thought, Fuck this." Vivian quickly puts her hand up to her mouth, as if she's horribly embarrassed. I couldn't help but laugh, couldn't even try not to. And as she looks back at me, it's like she suddenly remembers that it's just me, and she starts laughing too, like she told a dirty joke.

After we finish our sandwiches, I remind Vivian that I can stay all afternoon. I've told her repeatedly that I'm volunteering over my ten hours a week, that I really like helping her, especially now when there's so much to do. She seems careful not to expect the extra help, so every time it comes up, I have to remind her again that I want to be there. I really love the time at her house, not just in the garden, but whenever I take Buddy for a walk too. When you ask him if he wants to go for a walk, he tilts his head to the side, like he can't believe his ears. It's very endearing.

I decide to check my messages. Kay and I had talked about having dinner tonight, so I figured I'd see if she had decided yet. I had two voicemails from Rita at her boutique, so I was excited to check them. If more hats have sold, maybe we could go out. Her tone was almost fussy, like she was put out that I hadn't answered the phone, and her message just said to call her back. The tone was the same on the second message. "Cate, I need you to call me right away. There's a big problem. Just about every hat I have sold has been returned in the past two days. The beaded jewelry is falling apart. The same thing is happening with the ones that are still in the store. I don't know how you run your business, but this is certainly not how I run mine. Call me."

I hung up reflexively, trying to make the information stop, without listening to my other voicemails. I sat on the couch for a minute, trying to gather my thoughts. Buddy took this as his cue to come visit, sitting on the floor beside me with his head on my knee. I felt like I couldn't move or think straight either, for that matter. A few minutes later Vivian walked in. "Are you ok?"

"I'm fine." I answered, not meaning to lie. "Want to smoke?" I asked.

"Sure." She answered, before adding, "Maybe then you'll tell me what bee got into your bonnet."

As soon as we got outside, and I lit my cigarette, I told her about the message. "I don't know how this could have happened." I said, wondering if there was the slightest possibility that the hats at the other boutique were fine, or any way that I could fix the ones that weren't.

"Why don't you go ahead and call her back?" Vivian said. "Maybe it's not as bad as you think."

As soon as I finished my cigarette, I called her back, hoping Vivian could be right. She answered the phone on the first ring. "I got your message," I said, "I'm so sorry. I don't know how this could have happened. How many of the hats have been returned?"

"Almost all of them," she answered, but her tone was much softer than it had been on the voicemail.

"I'm sure I can figure it out and fix them." I said with more confidence than I felt.

"I don't think that's going to be an option. I've already refunded their money." There was a brief pause before she continued. "I'm going to need to get the money from those checks back from you."

My mind was reeling. I had already spent the money on more supplies, but I had to make this right. "Of course." I said, trying to come up with a solution while I still had her on the phone. "Do you think there's any way I can fix the hats that I haven't sold?" I asked, trying not to sound as desperate as I felt, realizing that I'm grasping at straws.

"I'm sorry." She answered, "My clientele is very picky, and I just can't take a chance on it. I don't know how to tell you this, but when I went over to check the ones in the display window, the beads started falling off as soon as I removed them from the hats. Without the beads, well, they're just hats with fabric."

"I am really sorry. I'll get you a check right away." In my head I was already wondering how I would pay bills next month, since that was the only money I had.

"I'm going to be out of town for the rest of the week. If you want to come by Monday with a check, that'll be fine."

"Thank you, and once again, I apologize. I'll be by Monday." I hung up the phone and was grateful to see Vivian standing in the door way. I hoped she had heard the conversation, so I wouldn't have to repeat it.

"It's not good." I said, before getting up and walking back out to the deck for another cigarette.

She followed me out there, and sat in her chair beside me. "Whatever it is, we'll figure it out." I could hear the mother in her voice. She had said this many times before. When I started to tear up, she said, "It will all be fine in the end. If it's not fine, it's not the end."

"It feels like my last chance though, my last chance at getting my life right. I know that sounds stupid, but it feels true. It took so long for me to get the hats right to begin with, and it turns out they weren't right after all. I wonder if that's why I couldn't feel really excited about them. At first I tried and tried to bead them with the metal wire, and it wouldn't bend right. When I found the clear plastic in your trunk, I thought I'd finally figured it out. And it worked so well, I thought it had been serendipitous."

Vivian didn't say anything. I figured she was thinking I sounded foolish, when she asked, "What are you talking about? What plastic in the trunk?"

"The trunk you had with the old clothes. That's where I found the stuff to bead them on, when you were at your retreat." Vivian's face was blank, like she had no idea what I was talking about. "You know, the trunk that had your old dresses and shoes in it? It looked like something you would use to string popcorn at Christmas."

Her mouth fell into an O shape. "That's what you used to make the necklaces?" I suddenly felt that my brilliant idea had in actuality been remarkably stupid, even though I couldn't see how or why. "That stuff has been in there for twenty years."

"But, it's plastic. Plastic lasts forever, at least that's what they said on Earth Day. It was on Oprah."

Vivian lit a cigarette. "Honey, those were stitches, dissolvable stitches. You know Walt worked up until when he died. I cleaned out his office. When I found those in his medical bag, I saved them because I thought they would work for holding a hem while I stitched with thread. They did. They worked better than pins. Oh, my word."

I sat there, trying to comprehend it, but I couldn't gather my thoughts cohesively. My mind was over powered by the feeling that I was a fraud. I couldn't do anything, couldn't make anything, wasn't worth a damn. I've done some remarkably dumb things before, and had to wonder, how could I be so stupid? This time there was no question. All I could think was I *am* so stupid.

CHAPTER 18

Dear Oprah,

Today I would give anything to go to your house, crawl into a fluffy bed, and sleep until my life looks different.

Regards,

Cate

P.S. If there is any chance of that ever happening, it would be a good time to let me know.

Despite Vivian's efforts to console me, I had to get out of there. If I didn't, I would never leave and hide at her house forever. I was torn between utter defeat and the necessity of salvaging the mess that I had made of my life. The defeat was winning when I thought of the money I had to return.

As soon as I found myself sitting on my condo floor, fighting back tears, I decided to call Jill to meet for drinks. We went to the pub near her house. By the time Jill walked in the door, I had already finished a martini.

I told Jill what happened, how I didn't have anything left. The money I had to repay could only come from my 401k. I would have to cash it out at the worst possible time, when it was worth a fraction of what I had put into it. This was the only way I could pay next month's bills, buying myself about four weeks to come up with another plan.

"I'm sure the other boutiques will want their money back too, after I give it all back, then I have a month to figure something out. I swear if my body was up for it, if I didn't have cellulite on my thighs, I would strip."

Jill's eyes widened. "Let's not go to extremes…"

"I can't go to that extreme if I want to, I'm too fat."

"You only have to give the money back for the hats that are returned, right?"

"Yeah, but I already thought about that. They'll all be returned sooner than later. It's inevitable. I need to go ahead and make it right now."

Jill picked at the corner of the label on her beer bottle, but it was glued on pretty well and wouldn't budge. "I know at least fifteen of them won't be returned."

It wasn't until I saw the guilty look on her face that I realized what she meant. She was the person who had bought my hats as gifts, my big surge in sales. I started to tell her that she shouldn't have, that they were all crap and going to fall apart, but there was no point. She knew that as well as I did. My dear friend had found a way to invest in me despite my protests of independence. "You know, you have the ones I bought to work with, to fix and start over."

That was the moment I knew that I didn't want to start over. I had clung to an idea that didn't fit me anymore than marketing or anything else I had done. I had been desperate and lost my faith that the right thing would present itself. Even if I could find a way to make a go of it, it would be at the wrong thing. I promised Jill that I would pay her back as soon as I could get on my feet, because after all, eventually you have to land on your feet. I think.

I lay in bed that night, wondering what the big joke was, and if it was me. I had counted on divine intervention to lead the way, and there had been none, only the pathetic attempts I had made to create something. I wondered how God sees us. I imagine it's like watching ants. They go back and forth, always appearing to be focused on a mission. Then one kid with a stick comes along and ruins their whole world, life as they know it in the castles that they've built and whatever treasure they have deep below them. Then it occurs to me that maybe that's exactly what it's like, and we are indeed the ants. Except there is no kid, maybe God is actually the one with the stick. Right now my wobbling hope and a prayer is all I have, so I should probably spend my time trying to fortify it.

The next day I made the necessary phone calls to empty my 401k. There was sixteen hundred dollars left in it, after the taxes and fees were deducted. I called the other boutiques and made arrangements to pick up the remaining hats and return their money. I wanted to wallow in self pity, and I would have if I had thought it wouldn't make the situation worse. As it was, I had very little money, no plan, and a small amount of time to come up with one.

After I had done everything I could for the day, I went to Vivian's. When I walked in I could smell fresh coffee and bacon. She was sitting at the table, about to eat her breakfast. "Hey, honey," she greeted me. "I didn't know if you'd make it over today or not. Go ahead and fix yourself a plate, we'll have breakfast together." Buddy looked back and forth, his tail wagging, like he'd just found out we were having a party.

I couldn't stomach food, but I poured myself a cup of coffee and sat down. "Today is going to be fun!" She announced. For a second I forgot about my problems and believed her. "The moonvines have gotten tall enough and strong enough that it's time for you to untangle them and start guiding them up the deck. It's just the kind of activity you need to relax and take your mind off things."

I was grateful that Vivian has this way about her. She doesn't make you talk about anything if you don't want to, and doesn't have it in her head that you should talk about every little thing anyway. Some people think the only way to deal with something is to talk it to death. I don't know what I believe, but this is so much nicer.

When she finished her breakfast we sat outside while we finished our coffee. Buddy sat on my feet, like he had sat on Vivian's the morning her friend died. I rubbed his head, thinking that for a dog that supposedly isn't that smart, he's got a keen heart that knows when someone needs extra attention. The weather was nice and warm, low eighties. I felt relaxed, even though there wasn't a reason on earth for me to be comfortable. After sitting in silence while we drank our coffee, Vivian said, "Cate, you'll figure it out." She winked at me before adding; "Now why don't you tend to those moonvines?"

Sure enough, they had gotten very tall. I had been carefully watering them every time I was here, seeing their progress. I guess it was all the spring sunshine we had had, but they seemed to have gotten significantly taller over the last week. Part of it also being that as they get taller, they are able to get more sun.

I didn't need Vivian to explain my task to me; I could see what she meant. Some of them had gotten wound up in each other. If they had been untangled sooner, the upward pull on them could have been too much. They had needed to dig their roots in. I was careful to unwrap them from each other, and give them each a different rung on the deck railing to hold onto instead. It was amazing to see how tall they were when they weren't wrapped around each other. I went from moonvine to moonvine, not thinking about anything other than guiding their growth. I was half way around the deck before I realized that I was praying.

I had confessed everything, how I had said I was going to have faith, but had really tried to control everything along the way. I expressed contrition for the doubt I had the night before, with a qualifying statement about how I wasn't sure it wouldn't creep back in when I was all alone. I asked for forgiveness, and realized that I was already forgiving myself. I forgave myself for not believing whole heartedly, for being scared, for being human. And unlike any feeling I've ever had in church, I knew it was ok. Peace like a river attendeth my soul.

It occurred to me that maybe I could stay and garden until I won the lottery, although I have only bought two tickets in my entire life. In my mind, a more likely scenario to hope for was that Oprah would adopt me after all. I felt like I didn't have anything else to hope for, so maybe it would happen. And unlike all the times I dreamt of it before, this time, I was hoping for it.

After a few hours, Vivian was done for the day. She asked if I wanted to come in for lunch, but I still wasn't hungry. I stayed out there and pulled weeds. I pulled the little weeds that come up easily and the strong ones that fight back before letting go of the earth, collecting them in a bucket so they wouldn't spread seeds from lying on the ground. I pulled and pulled until the sides of my fingers were raw from the tug of war. I would have pulled weeds until the sun set if Vivian hadn't come to get me.

"Your phone has been ringing." It must have been obvious that the phone wasn't a compelling incentive to get me to come inside because she added, "Besides, you can't keep pulling weeds. You're going to have blisters as it is."

I had two voicemails, one from Christian, asking if I wanted to go out for sushi, the other from Lainey, asking me to call her back when I got a minute. I really didn't want to talk to anyone, so I texted Christian back saying I'd have to take a rain check. I thought it was odd that Lainey had called me. I hadn't seen her since the night I had everybody over to Vivian's. Then I remembered, her friend Rita, the boutique owner. This made her both the last person I wanted to talk to and the one person I had to call back.

I left Vivian's and called her on the way home, wanting to get it over with. She answered on the first ring, dashing my hope of leaving her a message. "Hey, are you at home?" She asked.

"No, I'm heading there now. I just left Vivian's."

"Ok," she said, "I'll meet you there in thirty."

She hung up before I could say anything. Here's something I know for sure, even when you are no stranger to embarrassment, it doesn't mean that you're immune to it.

Within minutes after I got home, Lainey was at the door. I had already opened a bottle of wine to take the edge off of the inevitable confrontation. She walked in, and upon seeing my glass said, "Thank God for wine, pour me a glass too, will ya?" This was already less painful than I imagined. "Please tell me you have cigarettes too."

I grabbed a pack from the drawer and we headed to my balcony. "Lainey, I'm really sorry," I started. "I hope this didn't embarrass you or hurt your relationship with Rita in any way."

Lainey exhaled and tilted her head to the side. "What are you talking about?"

Her face was expressionless except for her slightly raised eyebrows. I was both stunned and grateful that she didn't know yet. Then I realized that I would have to be the one to tell her. I didn't want to ruin her visit just yet, so I stalled for time. "Oh, I'll tell you in a minute. What brings you over today?" I asked like this was the most natural thing in the world, like I'd just walked out onto Sesame Street.

"Cate, what's going on? What do you mean by you hope you didn't embarrass me?"

Since she wasn't going to let me put off telling her, I didn't have a choice. I started at the beginning, and told her everything. When I got to the part where Vivian told me that I had used dissolvable stitches, Lainey eyes widened, and then she laughed.

"I'm so sorry." I said, more than a little confused. Lainey kept laughing, and tears started to run down her cheeks.

When her laughter subsided she said, "I'm so sorry that happened. I really am, and I'm sorry I laughed, but why are you apologizing to me?"

"Because you know Rita. You got my foot in the door. I'm afraid I made us both look bad."

"You think Rita cares? I have known her for years. I promise you there is nothing to worry about with her. She has made plenty of snafus in her day."

"Really?" That didn't seem possible to me. This woman was polished and put together. She didn't have the mannequin quality like Alexis, but she was certainly nothing like me. I'm pretty confident that Rita can wear a white shirt without having traces of whatever she eats or drinks on the front of it by noon.

"Really. Let me tell you something. A few years ago we were invited to this big fancy Christmas party in Asheville. Me and Rita were out on the balcony smoking, and…"

"She smokes?"

"Yes, ma'am. She may only smoke when she drinks or be a closet smoker, but I've seen her light up plenty of times. Well anyway, Andie MacDowell was there." Lainey must have seen the question in my face before I could interrupt to ask. "Yes, the actress, Ground Hog Day Andie MacDowell, who by the way is the prettiest woman I have ever met. They had space heaters on the balcony, but it was still cold, so everyone was all bundled up. Including Andie MacDowell, who had her back to us, talking to some people we didn't know. Now Rita was pretty tipsy at this point, laughing and carrying on. She had been holding her cigarette like this." Lainey folded one arm across her chest, and held the elbow of her other arm with the cigarette, which was sticking out like she was miming a little tea pot. "Apparently she had held it up against the back of Ms. MacDowell's fur coat, at least that's what we figured out when it caught fire!" Lainey started laughing again.

"Then what happened?"

"Of course Rita was mortified. I mean mor-ti-fied. But after Andie MacDowell got the coat off, she laughed about it, assuring Rita that it was just a coat. That was that. My point is, don't worry about her. I've seen her at some of her finer moments." I sat there, relieved, forgetting momentarily that the dilemma that was my life still remained. "You thought that's why I was coming over here? Bless your heart."

The question lingered in the air, why Lainey had come over. It was her turn to stall. She went inside and grabbed the wine. When she returned she filled our glasses and said, "I need your help. I have to figure out how to fix this thing with Michael. When I fix things will Michael, when I make it right, I can mend things with Kay."

I suddenly felt drained. "Oh Lainey," I said, "I don't think I can."

"You think it's too far gone?"

"No, it's not that at all. In case you haven't noticed lately, everything I touch turns to shit. I don't know how I could help. I'd probably do more harm than good."

"That's not true…"

"Yeah, it is." I interrupted. "Really, all I want to do right now is order a pizza and watch reruns of Gilmore Girls on Lifetime in my pajamas, but I can't even afford to order a pizza."

It seemed watching Gilmore Girls was more troubling than my desire to be a hermit. "Why would you watch Gilmore Girls?"

"Because even though the way they talk irritates the crap out of me, they have a nice cozy life, with good food and old movies. And even though it makes me sick to hear Lora Li go on and on about how she doesn't want her parents' money, it's a ridiculous fictional world that I can get lost in. A world where financial relief is available to someone, and there is the option to refuse it because of some principles, misguided or otherwise."

"Aye, aye, aye. Cate, let me help. We can help each other. Why don't we make a list and see what we can fix together?"

"It's too late for me. I have no options, nothing left. I realize that life is going on for you and not to be dramatic, but I'm at the end of my rope. Everything is more than overwhelming, it actually is too much for me." As soon as I said it, I felt relief. My shoulders relaxed, and I let out a deep sigh. It was as if my despair was the truth, coming out after months of faked optimism. This was it, the real deal. I was an absolute mess, and it felt liberating to drop the charade.

"And I'm sorry Lainey, I know you came over wanting a solution, but I can't pretend that I'm ok anymore. I have to tell you, it feels good to admit it."

"Cate, I'm not dismissing or ignoring anything that you just said, but you do have an option. You can go back to marketing."

I took a long slow sip of my wine and shook my head. "I wish I could tell you that I won't do that, that I am out here on faith, but while I'm being honest…I'm not a Gilmore Girl with her principles. There aren't any jobs out there. I already looked." I relaxed further. Every piece of honesty was more liberating. It was like I had been weighed in front of the world, and could finally quit sucking my stomach in, pretending to be a size I wasn't.

"I'm sorry to dump all of this on you, but I have to finally be honest. You know, after everything happened with James I told him I'd rather have the ugly truth than a sweet lie. Then when he told me everything, why he cheated, I thought the truth was worse, but I was wrong. This, the truth, feels so much better."

Lainey finished her glass of wine and went home. I apologized again, but she said there was no need, that she shouldn't have barged in on me like that anyway.

I felt deliriously refreshed. Really I just felt refreshed, but thought I was probably delirious since it didn't seem possible that I could feel anything but devastated. I had done more than look at marketing positions, I had looked for any job. The job market was scarce; despite all the time I worked in various restaurants in college, I couldn't even get a job waiting tables. I had nothing of value to sell. The things I had supposedly bought, my car, my condo, were worth less than I owed. Without a job, I couldn't get a loan, or a line of credit.

There was nothing I could do about my situation tonight, if there was anything to do at all. It occurred to me that maybe the reason I was finally at peace with my situation, was that I was officially unraveling. The only unpleasant thought that accompanied letting myself lose it, was worrying the people who cared about me and imposing on whomever would let me sleep on their couch. As I enjoyed my new found ability to let go, I realized that what I had finally lost was my pride. Maybe I had bowed under the pressure of it. But now that it was gone, when it seemed I had everything to lose, the very release of it made me realize that I had everything to gain.

I opened another bottle of wine and turned the TV on. I soaked it in, only mildly aware that at the rate things were going, I wouldn't have cable much longer. I watched the ridiculously so-called reality shows, where girls don't have to have a job, a function. I laughed to myself about the irony: these girls were getting paid more than what used to be my annual salary per episode, to live their fake lives, going out carefree in the evenings, and with endless "job" opportunities in front of them.

One show led to another, until it was time for The People's Choice Awards. I opened another bottle of wine, not caring that I was already drunk. When the award show came on, I saw the excess of it all. One celebrity after another strolled down the red carpet, the same celebrities who were making hundreds of millions of dollars a year according to People Magazine.

Beyonce performed. I knew the song, and caught myself doing my own version of her video as a couch dance, moving only from the waist up. She made being a single lady sound so much better than it actually was. When she won an award, I clapped for her. I've bought all of her CDs, and thought she definitely deserved to win. "Thank you so much" she said, in that honey voice of hers. "This is such an honor, and I wouldn't be here tonight, if it weren't for you, supporting me." She gave a small bow with her head before exiting the stage.

I had supported her. I was one of the people she was thanking. It hit me that what little money I once had, had gone to support others. I had loyally supported Belvedere Vodka, Firestone Vineyards, and Victoria's Secret. I had supported the entire cast of Friends. When the show first came out, I had the wall calendar and a coffee mug. For years after I supported Jennifer Aniston at ten dollars per movie. I personally advertised for Virginia Slims every time I had my cigarettes sitting out on a bar. It dawned on me that I wasn't just a consumer. I knew the wine was coloring my thoughts, but it seemed a fact that I had indeed been a supporter.

Here I was, supporting all of these entities, not always getting much in return. How many times had Victoria's Secret let me down, promises of sexiness that only resulted in my wearing an uncomfortable, unflattering contraption? I thought of all the CDs I bought that only had a few good songs, the bad movies I had sat through, the bottles of wine that had been acidic.

I got out my laptop and wrote a letter to Beyonce. I had supported all of these people in their endeavors, why wasn't I asking them to support me? It was perfectly logical. I couldn't believe it hadn't occurred to me before. I couldn't stop myself. I sent letter after letter to celebrities, outlining my support and asking for a little in return.

I told Jennifer Aniston how I had always been on her side and added that she was superior to Angelina Jolie. I went from website to website, easy to navigate since my shopping loyalty was evident by the websites saved as favorites.

I poured another glass of wine, squinting to make out my own typing. Jennifer Aniston made me think of Brad Pitt, and I grew indignant on both of our behalf. I found his fan website and sent an email to him too. Although a lot of his movies have been subpar, I was only asking that he return what I had paid for Meet Joe Black. This is the last thing I remember doing that night.

CHAPTER 19

Dear Oprah,

I have no idea what to do with my life, but this is for certain: I'm going to need Bob Greene to get my ass in shape. I've had so much wine and frozen food in the past two months that I can't fit into any of my jeans. And at the rate things are going, if I'm going to keep anything, it will have to be my looks. They never seemed like quite the prize before, but I certainly can't afford to lose them if they're really all I've got left.

Regards,

Cate

Ps. I realize that I may not seem like the most likable choice for an adoptee, but I am still available.

I awoke the next morning on my couch with a pounding headache. As I strained to focus my eyes, it wasn't hard to figure out why. The empty bottles were on the coffee table. I got up, trying to collect my thoughts and repair the disaster area that was my condo. It was official. I had become a complete mess.

The smell of the red wine left in my glass made me gag when I poured it down the drain. I didn't feel like showering, but between the empty pint container of Ben & Jerry's on my coffee table, and the stickiness in the ends of my hair, I gathered that I didn't have a choice. I looked at the carton in a haze, vaguely remembering that I had written a letter to Ben about my loyal support of his ice cream.

I had voicemails, another from Rachel from my old office, reminding me that I had never called her back. Kay had called, twice. It was only noon. Since when was I so popular? There was a voicemail from Vivian too, checking on me. *Shit*, I thought, remembering I told Vivian I would be over early today.

Oprah leaves her houseguests water, aspirin, and Gatorade by their beds. This definitely wouldn't have happened there. I took some Advil, my gag reflex kicking in again as I tried to swallow them, and got into the shower.

When I walked into Vivian's I could smell something fried, the way grease lingers in the air. She was standing at the stove, Buddy sitting at her feet, eager to catch anything that might drop. "Hey, honey," she greeted me, not a trace of irritation that I was three hours late. Before I could apologize she said, "Don't be sorry, you're such a big help, I only called to make sure you were alright."

"I didn't mean to worry you." I said, remembering how badly I used to feel on the rare occasion when I would come home late in high school and see that my mom wasn't able to sleep because of it.

"I wasn't worried, just wanted to check. I thought you might need a break and want to stay home today." Her eyes surveyed me slowly, undoubtedly noting the circles under my eyes, the water retained in my face. She asked me to hand her the plate she had on the counter with the paper towel on it. She took it from me and starting lifting lovely little breaded circles out of the pan and placing them on it.

"Fried green tomatoes," she said, "Have one, you need to eat something. I make them every spring, when the tomatoes get big, and I can't wait for them to ripen to start picking!" We ate a few, and then went out back.

Normally this is when Vivian and I talk about life, but today she handed me a piece of paper as soon as we sat down. Her hand writing was small, dainty, and I couldn't figure out if it was hard to read or if that was a result of my hangover. "Pardon my chicken scratch."

There they were, the elusive secrets on paper. It outlined all the vegetables and flowers in the garden, with detailed instructions on how to tell when something was ready to be picked. By the line that read 'sweet potatoes' it simply said, 'You'll know, they'll start to push the ground up beneath them.'

I smiled, despite my state, "You finally decided to write some of this stuff down," I said. She nodded. Buddy came over to where I was sitting and licked my hand. Even though bending forward made my head throb, I hugged his thick fuzzy black neck. He muzzled his wet nose into my neck.

When we went into the garden she showed me where she had placed more of her copper garden markers. The garden looked organized, labeled, and as beautiful as ever. I knew why she loved spring most. It was incredible to see all of our hard work coming up through the ground. I began tending to my moonvines. Before too long, I was so glad that I had come, grateful that I had something to help me forget.

I stayed until dinner time. Vivian was having Betty over for supper and I didn't want to intrude on their mother-daughter time. I knew I needed some sister time, so I went to Kay's, who luckily was happy to have me. When I walked in I was surprised to see Lainey sitting on her couch. It was only a fleeting thought that I was going to have to apologize everywhere I went that day, before I realized that I should be glad Lainey had Kay and wasn't relying on the likes of me for support.

"Lainey, I'm sorry." I said, "I don't know what happened to me last night. I guess I had to let go, regardless of what was going on around me."

She got up and hugged me, whispering "Thank you." in my ear.

"For what?" I asked, wondering if she had somehow missed how unhelpful I had been.

"You told me exactly what I needed to hear. You were right, the ugly truth is better than a sweet lie. Today I told the ugly truth. I did it. I told Michael everything. I didn't make a single excuse for what I did, even when I explained why."

"Oh shit." I said. Lainey sat back down on the couch, and Kay sat beside her.

"It was the right thing to do." Lainey said. "He didn't tell me that it was ok, and his lawyer will probably have a field day with it, but that's fine. Maybe someday he'll forgive me, but it felt better to tell the truth. It didn't feel good, but it felt better."

Kay made dinner, and Lainey and I spent the night. It felt like a slumber party for family, for the people you need to have around you when it's too hard to be alone. And sometimes that is all you need.

The next morning I reluctantly went home. Lainey had to go to meet with her divorce lawyer; bracing him for the nail in the divorce coffin that Michael's divorce attorney would soon deliver. I made my coffee from a can, realizing that I needed to be grateful to have any coffee at all. I tried to make a list for the grocery store, since my pantry and fridge were bare. I couldn't bring myself to clip coupons, like I had been.

There is a level of broke where every penny counts. You will do whatever you can to save twenty cents here and seventy five cents there, knowing that every single cent matters. The greater level of broke is when there isn't a penny that matters. You could spend a nickel or a hundred dollars. If you have neither, there is no difference between them. I had one month to get my shit together, and there was no way to ration out any of it for more time.

I checked my email, before heading to the store, resigned to the defeat of my situation. For a split second, I remembered the drunken emails I had sent, and had a flicker of long shot hope that there would be some grand response saving the day. Of course, there was none. My inbox was filled with sale offers for things I wouldn't be buying, and the usual spam for honeymoon contests that I had entered. As I checked the little boxes to delete them, I noticed that I had an email from John, from my old office.

Even as I read the good news, I couldn't muster more than a little sigh of resignation. God had made a way. It wasn't what I had thought it would be. I didn't find my purpose after all, but it was something. In the five months since I had been laid off, they had discovered that Barbara was taking credit for my work. She had been using my old projects as her new ideas, and had only been able to peddle them so far before it was obvious to him. They were letting Barbara go and offering me my old job back.

I tried to feel good about it. I would have a job. I wouldn't have to go into foreclosure and get kicked out of my condo, or spend the next month trying to find odd jobs to make ends meet in the off chance I could prevent that from happening. It was disheartening to think I had done all of this to end up where I started, minus my savings or 401k, but I knew I had to be grateful. Sometimes you accept that you don't have to see the lesson to know that you have learned one.

With a little hope in my heart, I skipped the store and went to Vivian's. With spring came daily watering, and if my time was going to be limited soon, I wanted to enjoy what I had left. I was surprised to see Betty's car in the driveway. I guess you're never too old for slumber parties. When I walked in, Buddy ran to greet me. His tail wasn't wagging, but he almost knocked me over with the force of his weight when I bent down. I sat on the floor, rubbing his head before I noticed that the house was eerily silent. I got up to find Betty sitting at the kitchen table. There was a box of Kleenex in front of her.

I think you know which moments are going to matter to you, because you take stock of all the details, like what you're wearing while they're happening. I had on baggy green cargo pants and a white tank top, worn thin and dingy from wear. I could smell the coffee, and it felt like slow motion as Betty's head turned to look at me.

I knew the second she made eye contact. I had already felt Vivian's absence in the air. Even though she is Vivian's daughter, I knew I wouldn't be taking anything away from her grief as I sat back on the floor and cried. She knew I loved Vivian too. In a gesture that let me know that I was one who hadn't expected this, she came over and hugged me, sitting on the floor beside me. As soon as her arms wrapped around me, I began to sob. I knew I had lost the person who had become my dearest friend, my Vivian. Betty let me sit on the floor until my tears ran dry, my heart wrenched.

After what seemed like hours, Betty asked me if I wanted to go smoke, and led me out back to the deck.

She handed me Vivian's lighter and said, "You should have this." As my fingers traced over her engraved initials, new tears formed, and Betty let me cry in silence. Buddy came and sat on my feet. I realized that he needed comfort too, and tried to assure him it was going to be fine.

Betty brought me coffee, and I fought to compose myself, feeling sorry for her, that she had to deal with me on top of the death of her mom. "She knew it was her time…she's been making arrangements for a while." she said. "She left you a letter." Betty handed me an envelope. I opened it slowly. I was desperate for one last word from Vivian, but knowing that as soon as I read it there would be no more last words from Vivian. My hands were shaking, so I pressed it down on the table to steady the page.

There in her dainty print it read, "Dear Cate, You have been such a blessing to me. I feel lucky to have had you in my life, and have enjoyed every minute of our time together. You remind me so much of myself and that makes me feel good, because you are a wonderful person. Things look different at the end of your life than they do at all of the beginnings. You can see the forest through the trees. I wanted to tell you some time ago that I figured out what you should do with your life, but it never felt like the right time. I didn't know if you should come to it on your own. You're a plant girl. The peace you feel in the garden, that's your sign, honey. You don't have to make a life out of it if you don't want to, but it's yours if you'd like it. I love you. Vivian"

As soon as I finished I read it again. "She left it where all you have to do is sign to have the house and business transferred into your name." Betty said. "We talked about it some time ago. She asked me how I felt about it, and I thought it was perfect. If you don't want the house and the garden…"

Betty didn't get to finish her sentence. I hugged her hard, and said "I want it." There was nothing to think about, only questions, which I was too overwhelmed to ask.

"She did have a favor to ask you." Betty looked down at Buddy.

"I want him too!" I cried, wondering how that could ever be a favor, or a question.

"Don't you want it, the house, the garden…?" I asked.

"No." Betty shook her head. "This isn't my life. It never has been. It was mom's. She wanted you to have it, and I do too." She squeezed my hand, and I knew she meant it.

CHAPTER 20

Dear Oprah,

I'm sorry about the letter I sent about the end of your show. And I'm sorry about the emails after that, for anytime I questioned your choice in doing that. It was selfish and self absorbed, and I'm ashamed to say that I meant every word when I sent it. But I've changed. I am happy for you. You came into your OWN, and I know I will always look forward to your next chapter. Look at how far we've come. I'm in the right place for me, and I am confident that you're moving in the right direction for you.

Yours,

Cate

Ps. Although I'm no longer seeking adoption, I am always available to hang out. If you ever want to come by for a glass of wine and watch the moonvines, let me know.

Vivian told me once that life works out when you're not trying to do the work for it. At the time it was hard for me to believe, because I was fighting with myself, my fate, trying to create something that was there all along. I miss Vivian every single day. Whenever I'm overcome with emotion and wishing she was still here, I try to think about what Oprah would say about grieving. Oddly the only thing that comes to mind is something my Grandaddy once told me. You can wish in one hand and shit in the other. You'll see whch hand gets full first.

I moved into the house, which despite what I had expected, never felt strange. I rented out my condo, which will have to due until the market picks up and I can sell it. The garden doesn't bring in a lot of income, but the house is paid for, so it brings in enough. It's enough to live comfortably and to have the good coffee.

The best part of all is that when I'm in the garden, I know I'm exactly where I'm supposed to be in my life. Whether it's picking the vegetables and bringing them to the market, or trying to make my own preserves the way Vivian used to, I'm at peace. Dinner with Christian is still as close as I have gotten to a date, but I will, when I'm ready.

Tonight I'm having the girls over. Kay has started seeing someone new. She's been stingy with the details, but that is usually a good sign with her. Love. Kay gives it selflessly and I know it's coming back to her. Maybe not this guy, but soon.

Jill is working on being happy on her own. I know she's struggling, but now it can be my turn to be supportive. Reciprocity. I wonder if Oprah and Gayle yo-yo with each other like that.

Lainey is starting fresh in her life, from scratch after the divorce. She's happy and looking for a job. She is staying with me and Buddy until she gets on her feet. Providence. I finally live in a place big enough to offer a friend a place to stay.

The moonvines have just started blooming. I can see why Vivian didn't tell me about them. She didn't want to ruin the surprise. After the months of guiding them as they seem to weave endlessly around the deck, they form long buds on the end. Then, like magic, one night when the sun goes down and the moon shows up, a flower blooms. They're big, stark white, delicately intricate but sturdy at the same time. They look like they're made out of fabric. My favorite thing in the whole world is to sit on the back deck with a glass of wine, and wait for the exact moment when the sun goes down and the bloom opens. Watching them reminds me how I want to live my life. If you take the time, you'll see the most enchanting things.

It was bittersweet. The day Vivian died was the day I realized my purpose. I guess she had a people thumb too. I framed her garden instructions, so they'll always be preserved, and I can't spill anything on them. I've already made some mistakes, but I'm learning and enjoying every minute of it.

I don't know how I missed it when she first handed them to me, but at the bottom, after she's listed how to care for zucchini, yellow squash, and egg plants, there were instructions for how to care for myself too. She wrote: You – room to breathe, moments to enjoy the moonvines, and the morning glories, time to feel the earth, and grow and blossom.

Epilogue

Dear Beyonce,

Congratulations on your win at The People's Choice Awards. You deserve it and were my choice. During your acceptance speech, you thanked your fans and said you wouldn't have been there without their support. I am one of the people who has supported you. I can't tell you how many of your CDs I have bought, and more recently downloaded from ITunes. I even went to see your movie, Obsessed. (For the record I have also supported Jay-Z. I loved his interview with Oprah.) I have identified with you, and your love of fried chicken, but tonight when you were singing Single Ladies, I felt like you may not realize what it is like for the rest of us, who really are single ladies. We are not going on private yachts to private islands for vacation. We are trying to muster up thirty dollars for a few glasses of wine out with our friends. It's not easy. We're trying to go somewhere to do the Single Ladies dance (btw, great video!), and it's hard to fund the entertainment. I have truly supported you, and even defended you when others have begrudged you your success. And I've been happy to do it. But let me tell ya, being independent is a hard road to travel in real life. I am struggling. I have tried to start my own business, only to find that it's hard to make a solid go of anything without money behind it. You got a big head start on me, always knowing what you wanted to do and having a boat load of talent. If you truly believe that you wouldn't be where you are today without the support of your fans, I'm unabashedly asking you to repay the favor and support me in my business favor. That's not true; I'm semi-mortified to be sending this email. As it is, there is no room for any pride, and I would be truly grateful for any assistance whatsoever.

Regards,
Cate

Dear Virginia,

I have been smoking Virginia Slims for years, and years. Even after many friends have quit smoking, I have remained a true and loyal customer. Whenever I am at a bar, I have my cigarettes visibly present in the packaging. Essentially I have provided free advertising for your brand for eight years. I have also aided in distribution, as I have purchased your cigarettes from vending machines as well, which has to be noticeable when they are restocked. I have not asked for anything in return, with the exception of my enjoyment of your product. However, times have changed and money is tight. I have continued to purchase your product despite the ever increasing expense associated with it. I will not sue you if I develop problems from not heeding the warning on your cigarette, thus costing you time, money, and inconvenience. As a valued customer I would like to ask that you return the favor and invest in me as well. I am broke. Broke, broke, broke. I need money for a start up business. Any help would be greatly appreciated.

Cate

P.S. I am switching to some additive free cigarettes, but that's not the point.

Dear Andrew Firestone,

Not only have I been a loyal customer of your family's wine, I watched you on The Bachelor. You were quite cute, and it was a pleasure to witness your dating extravaganza. However, unlike you, I do not have family resources to draw upon in a time of need. I have no money. I would desperately like to start my own venture, but so far that has not worked out very well as I have not been able to secure proper funding. Have you considered funding a grant program for those of us who are hard working and ambitious, but without financial means? If so, I would like to be first on the list for applications. As things are now, I will no longer be able to afford your Prosperity Merlot.

Regards,

Cate

P.S. If your Prosperity wine is supposed to bring fortune to those who drink it, it has not worked for me.

Dear Mr. Belvedere,

You were the best butler ever. I'm kidding. I have been drinking your vodka for years. It is my vodka of choice for martinis. I would use it for mixed drinks, but I can't afford it for everything. Which brings me to my little problem. I couldn't even count how many times I have spent fifty-six dollars for a bottle of your vodka. I use it at home, order it out, and have given it as gifts. There have been other, cheaper vodkas, which I haven't even tried for a martini because I have trusted that yours was the best. I would like for you to consider returning the favor and investing in me as well. I'm trying to start a business and have very little funds to further my endeavor. The smallest assistance would be greatly appreciated. Without some assistance I don't see how I can afford to remain the loyal customer I have been. However with your help I have every confidence that I can be a success and continue to purchase and promote your product. Your consideration is greatly appreciated.

Regards,

Cate

Dear Chelsea Handler,

I went to see you perform, and girl, you were drunk. I know that is part of your charm, and my support of your career probably affords you that option. That being said, would you like to contribute to my business venture? I'm making hats. This email would probably be more convincing, but I've been drinking. I'm sure you understand.

Regards,

Cate

P.S. Seriously, you were so fucking drunk. Could you at least send me the $86 I spent on the ticket?

Dear Jennifer Aniston,

I can't tell you how much I admire you. You've come a long way, and you have done it with such grace, you're like a mini white Oprah. I have a long way to go and hope I can do it with the same kind of dignity. As it is, I'm struggling. I watched you on Friends (but who didn't) and followed your career with trips to the movie theatre and DVD purchases. Along Came Polly was hysterical! And for the record, I know you have good friends like Courtney Cox and you don't need me telling you this, but Brad is an ass clown. He was quite the catch when you were with him, but after that it was all downhill in my book. Anyway, my point. I have supported you from the first season of Friends, and I'm so glad that so many people did and that you have been successful. I'm not succeeding right now. I'm trying, but nothing is going my way. I'm sure you know what that feels like. The thing is, my dad isn't a famous actor, and no one is going to bail me out of the shit I'm standing in. If there is any way that you would consider contributing what I know could be my future success, please let me know. I work hard, and I really need a break. I promise that if you invest in me, I will do whatever I can to give you a return and make something of myself.

Regards,

Cate

P.S. I will NEVER watch Mr. & Mrs. Smith. Also, if you're really friends with Chelsea Handler, can you get me a refund on the ticket I spent to see her? She was drunker than I am right now. Yowzah.

Dear Victoria,

Girl, I know your secret. You don't eat. For years I have bought panties that look more like contraptions with bands everywhere, and bras that are so uncomfortable they have sucked my will to live. And when you made a change to your brand, I had to have the word PINK on my ass, but I did it and wore your pajamas anyway. Do you know how many pink bags I've walked out of your store with over the years? I'm committed and loyal. Now I need some help. Unfortunately I can't sell my used bras and unflattering thongs, but with the amount of money I have spent, I need a return on my investment. So I'm asking you to invest in me. I'm a real girl, not some "angel" from your ads. Nobody is paying me a ton of money to show up and walk around in my underwear. And I'm broke. Seriously, I have given you so much of my income over the years with false hope that I will look sexy in it, and I need something back. I have started a business venture that is low on financial backing. Please consider me at the top of your list for financial contributions or charitable donations. And I won't tell anybody about your secret one way or the other because I'm not like that.

Regards,

Cate

P.S. Please quit saying that a certain style flatters every figure. Sometimes, they just don't.

Dear Brad Pitt,

You are an ass clown. Why you would ever leave Jennifer Aniston is beyond me. But on to other matters, I am broke. I would like my eight dollars back for Meet Joe Black. That was a colossal waste of my time, and I would like a refund.

Cate

Acknowledgements

Thank you to the following individuals who without their contributions and support this book would not have been written:

My husband Paul, who chose to make this journey with me. Questo è uno di quei momenti in cui mi sarà lieto che qualcosa è andato perso nella traduzione. Siete ancora la roccia del mio mondo.

My parents Carroll and Brenda, who never limited my imagination or my dreams. My sister Corey, who brings a special sister element to all of my writing and reads very rough drafts. My friend Courtney Mosteller, who was excited even when I was terrified. And Ben Rooke merits a special acknowledgement for reminding me of who I am. Ben, I took the left.

I have the greatest appreciation for some gifted writer friends: Andi Buchanan, Caroline Leavitt, Meg Waite Clayton and Jennifer Lauck. Despite busy schedules and their own work, they generously made time to share their expertise.

Oprah has inspired me to be my best self and pursue my authentic life. I hope she finds this book to be an homage to her.

And to everyone who has to start over, you can do it. And watching Oprah can help.

About the Author

Erin Emerson is a writer, living in Atlanta with her husband Paul and their mighty dogs.

www.ingramcontent.com/pod-product-compliance
Lightning Source LLC
Chambersburg PA
CBHW071128170626
46809CB00002B/533

9780615880488